Higher Love
Sentinel Security N.Y.C. Book 3

Eliza Renton

LOVE DESERVES A SECOND CHANCE

Six years ago, Mary disappeared without a trace, leaving Trigger shattered and vowing to never to open his heart again. When she suddenly reappears, desperate and on the run, his world dives into chaos. Determined to keep her at arm's length, he agrees to protect her. But Mary is hiding something—and the truth will change everything.

With a target on her back, Mary is out of options and out of time. Abandoning witness protection could cost her more than her life, but the man she left behind is the only person who can help her, even if he wants nothing to do with her.

As the danger intensifies, will they find a way to overcome the past, trust each other again, and survive, or will fear and betrayal rip them apart forever?

Acknowledgements

Thank you to my editors. Without you I'm sure this book would never have come to print. Any errors remaining in this book are all down to me. As always, my thanks to my writing group, The Saturday Ladies Bridge Club. Without your encouragement and wealth of knowledge I would be out there in the deep end swimming alone. And to the wonderful women in our Sit and Knit group. You keep me sane!

Contents

Chapter One

MOM USED TO SAY Spring made the sun pop blossoms on the trees to cheer up the parks. She enjoyed long walks in the rain. Mary, on the other hand, didn't share the love, and it had been pouring for the past five days.

You're a grump, Mary. Acting like a toddler whose parents refused to let their kid eat candy for breakfast. She was an adult. An underpaid social worker wrangling an ever-growing client caseload.

On her salary, she wasn't taking a first-class vacation any time soon. So what? As a single mom, she had no intention of giving up her job, even if a million dollars magically appeared in her bank account.

Picking up her pace, she cringed against the pelting rain and pulled the collar of her coat closer to her ears. She loved helping and supporting teenagers through the tough times. A fact she chose not to share with her coworkers. In case they thought she found Jesus or was a do-gooder Pollyanna. She didn't want to be *that* girl. The one who didn't get asked to join them at the bar on a Friday night.

Heading across town to her office, she hummed Happy Birthday to herself and smiled. Her favorite twenty-four hours of the year wasn't for a couple of days, but Matt promised he'd make it home in time to celebrate. After not seeing him for six months, already the week had been endless.

Remembering the last time he was on leave from his unit, her lips twitched. He barely made it through the door before she lost her panties, and the glad-to-see-you-honey-fun started. Matt called her gorgeous all the time, but in a few months, she'd look like a gigantic football.

Congratulations! You're pregnant! Her doctor had waved the results of the blood and urine tests in front of her and grinned. *Christ on a cracker.* After the first time they made love, Matt's arms surrounding her, his heart beating against her ear, he let it slip he didn't want children.

Of course, he meant not right now. Coz they were engaged. *Yeah, and he's away a lot.* Standing at the crosswalk, Mary jumped back to avoid the car wheels, splashing her legs with muddy water.

Would Matt dump her when he found out a kid was on the way? Because that would suck big time. Head over heels in love didn't come close to how she felt about him.

Kind, tick, caring, tick. Never doubted her, encouraged her to follow her dreams. Perfect. She couldn't imagine the sun shining on another day without him in her life.

It wasn't all on him. Was she ready to be a mother? She started work at six and often finished late at night. After going home and snacking on crackers and cheese some nights, she didn't have the energy to make it off the couch into bed. Unless Matt was home. He loved to take care of her. They ate out, or he cooked. Now, she'd need to eat for two.

Telling him he was going to be a dad ranked a ten plus on her anxiety scale. One night, that's all it took to turn her world upside down. Called out on an emergency, she'd missed taking the pill and the window for popping the morning-after option.

No babies. Stop, Mary. You're working yourself into a froth. Every girl has options. Nope. She wanted this baby even if she had to manage alone. Her stomach cartwheeled. "Ugh." Slumped against the wall of a shop, she did her best not to puke. Tears rolled over her cheeks. Damn hormones. She sniffed.

Lightning turned the sky purple, and thunder rolled overhead as the light turned green and flipped to red before she made it halfway across. Headlights raced toward her through the rainy mist.

"Get out of the damn way," a cabbie hollered.

Unsure whether to keep going or turn back, she froze. The handle of her pocketbook slipped from her shoulder when strong fingers gripped her elbow and dragged her across the street.

"You, okay," the man said. His huge, black umbrella tilted forward and drops of rain dripped onto the tip of her nose.

"Yes, thanks. Head in the clouds." Her arms wrapped protectively round her waist. "Sorry."

"What for? Hey, you're shivering. Wanna get a cup of coffee?"

Fantastic. The universe's gift to damsels in distress winked at her. Should she take off her glove and flash her engagement ring? "Love to, but I'm on my way to meet a friend. Thanks again. Have a great day." She waved and kept walking.

Pregnant. Damn. Matt deserved to know as soon as he got back from wherever it was the military sent him. That nagging voice in her head was back. What if he meant what he said and he couldn't hack being a father?

No more lying in bed until midday. Forget sleepy sex before breakfast. Diapers and saggy breasts were her immediate future.

Her tongue was hanging out for that coffee by the time she made it to the office. She loaded a new filter and waited for the machine to do its thing. "Last one, baby. We're going cold turkey after this. And don't worry." She patted her still flat belly. "Daddy is going to be over the moon when he hears about you."

Her phone buzzed in her pocket. Seeing as it was after six, she should ignore the call, but a client might be in trouble. "Mary Lane. How can I help?"

"It's Tilly."

The teenager's voice trembled. Something was wrong. "What's going on? Where are you?"

"At my gran's. He's here. That man, the one who has been hanging round my school. He followed me home."

Sleaze. Last week, Tilly called, scared out of her wits, because she was sure someone was following her. There was a restraining order against her father, banning him from being within a hundred yards of his daughter, but she wouldn't put it past him to send his cronies to grab her.

Naturally, Tilly hadn't wanted to go to the police. No kid wanted to believe their dad was a douchebag. "Is Gran home, Tilly?" This time of day, they were often in the kitchen making dinner.

"No. She left a note. She's gone to the store for eggs. What should I do? He's with another man, and they're sitting outside in the car."

"I'm on my way. Call the police and don't open the door until I get there." It wasn't far, one block over, across from the park.

"Hurry." Tilly choked.

"It's okay, just stay inside." Mary shoved her phone into her pocket and ran, praying the police were on their way. Her heart pounded in her ears.

The car was right where Tilly said, standing in front of her grandmother's house. The shiny, high-end sedans didn't look like something her father could afford to drive. "Slow down," she mumbled under her breath, and did her best to walk at a normal pace past the car.

Forcing herself not to look behind her, she kept moving down the block to the next corner before turning into a narrow alley that led to the lane at the rear of the houses.

Feeling lightheaded from the run, with a good dose of fear thrown in, she was lightheaded by the time she tried the handle of the back door. Locked, just like she'd Tilly. Only the airhead in the movies left it unlocked for the bad guys. And the teenager had years of street smarts under her belt.

"Tilly. It's Mary. Let me in." She kept her voice low and knocked softly. The door flew open, and Tilly sprang into her arms. Holding her close, she ushered them inside and nudged the door closed with her hip. "Are you okay? Where's Gran?"

"In there." Tilly nodded to the room at the end of the hall.

Slippers on her feet, a huge colorful shawl wrapped around her shoulders, Gran sat in an overstuffed armchair, watching TV. Nothing stopped for the afternoon game shows.

Mary shivered. The place was freezing, and a musty, damp smell tickled her nostrils. How long had they been without heat? Next time she was in the office, she'd get them some help to pay the heating bill.

A sudden thud followed by a loud crack sent her blood pressure soaring. Male voices echoed along the hallway. *Where the hell were the cops?*

"We can't wait any longer. Vokov is expecting us to show up with the girl in half an hour."

Oh, hell. A friend of Tilly's father. As far as her organization knew, a key player in an international child trafficking ring. "Hide." She waved at Tilly to duck behind her gran's chair and plastered her back against the wall.

"Please. Don't let them take me," Tilly whimpered.

The terrified teenager huddled next to her gran, who patted the top of her head. Deaf or mind-bogglingly unaware, she kept her eyes glued to the TV.

"You go upstairs while I check down here."

She couldn't see him, but the man speaking had a Slavic accent. "Is there another way out?" she whispered. Tilly shook her head and took a step toward her, sending the lamp on the side table flying. For less than a breath, time stood still, then hell broke loose.

The sound of the other man running back down the stairs made her made her blood run cold. Another few seconds and they would reach them.

"Go," Gran's frail fingers waved them toward the back door.

"No. I'm not leaving you," Tilly insisted.

"Take her, Mary. Go, now."

Adrenaline surged through her veins. She had no choice. The men were here for her granddaughter. Mary grabbed Tilly's hand, but didn't make it far before two men, dressed in black, their faces covered, crashed into the room.

Instinctively, one arm wrapped around her waist, shielding her baby, while she used the other to push the girl behind her. A hand covered in tattoos grabbed her hair and wrenched her away from Tilly. Stars crowded the edge of her vision.

Mary lashed out with her foot and whooped with nervous joy when her heel connected with the ape's groin. With a roar, he staggered backwards, then, *oh hell,* he charged. Her shoe caught on the frayed rug when she tried to avoid contact.

Her knee twisted underneath her, and a sharp pain shot up her thigh as she fell. Level with her now, her attacker raised his foot and stomped on her injured leg. *Far out.* This time, the stars zinging back and forth were a damn constellation.

"Payback's a bitch," he sneered.

Gritting her teeth and looking for something to use as a weapon, Mary staggered to her feet and was almost at the door when the man grabbed her arm, twisted it into the middle of her back, and pointed his gun at Tilly.

"Calm the fuck down. Or I put a bullet in the kid's brain."

Unlikely, considering the teenager was what they came for, but she daren't risk it. Any minute now, the cops had to arrive. *Make that now.*

"We're out of here. Move." The other man grabbed Tilly by the back of her neck and pushed her toward the door.

"No. Mary, please," Tilly screamed.

Grinding her teeth against the searing pain in her knee, she dragged a breath deep into her lungs. "It's okay, Tilly, I'm here. Do as he says."

"*Suka.*" The man holding her slapped her across the face.

In her career, she'd been called a bitch in many languages. She recognized the Russian insult. Swallowing the bloody saliva flooding her mouth, she raised her chin. "Leave her alone."

"Or what, *Suka?*"

Crazy possibilities raced through her head. Terrified, mad as hell, she answered with every cuss word she knew.

"Police. Freeze."

Her whole body shuddered. Patting her belly, she forced herself to stay calm. *It's okay, baby. Calvary's arrived.*

"Put down your weapons."

Hallelujah. The ape let go of her arm while the other pitched Tilly headfirst onto the ground. Both men opened fire. Mary grabbed Tilly's shirt, dragged her to Gran's chair, and threw her body over them, shielding them from the bullets whizzing over their heads.

The man who'd hit her made it to the door before the cop shot him. Lying on the ground, his lifeless eyes bored straight through her.

"Freeze," both officers yelled at the other guy as they chased him into the street. "Suspect heading east on foot. We need a medic at the house."

Sirens blared. *It's okay, baby. We're safe.* Mary stroked her belly and stood, but her injured knee had swollen to twice its size and was impossible to bend.

"Wow, that's gotta hurt," Tilly shouted.

Mary chuckled. The gunfire had been deafening, and Tilly hadn't taken her fingers out of her ears. "I'm okay." Mary smiled and eased Tilly's hands to her side. "They're gone."

"That knee doesn't look good. You need to go to the hospital," Gran said and rearranged her shawl.

Before she could tell her she planned on doing that, the officers returned.

"Anyone hurt?" the one who shot her attacker asked, his eyes zeroing in on her knee.

Mary shook her head. No comparison between her bruises and the gaping hole in the man's chest lying in the pool of blood two feet away.

"Paramedics are outside. Can you walk?" He turned to the other cop. "Joe? You got the other two?"

"I'm not going anywhere. You damn idiots broke my TV." Gran waved an arthritic finger at the cracked screen.

The cop blushed. Tilly rolled her eyes. The cut on her face needed attention.

"I'm good." Mary winced, waving him off. "Take care of Tilly." Her knee felt as though it had swallowed a block of wood, but the cop had his arm around Tilly now, so she limped beside him while Joe inspected Gran's TV.

Outside, he led them to the waiting paramedics. Suddenly, she felt hot and couldn't stop shivering. A woman in uniform threw a blanket over her shoulders. "Thanks." *Where are you, Matt? I need you.* He was probably on a plane, so there was no point in calling him.

"I'll leave you in Detective Cooper's hands," the cop nodded to someone behind her.

A man in dress pants and a dark blue jacket with yellow lettering on it. *FBI?* Sucking in a deep breath, Mary did her best to focus on what he was saying but couldn't make out a single word. Gulping for air, she burst into tears. "I'm pregnant."

Chapter Two

THE FLUORESCENT LIGHTS WERE driving her crazy. Between the constant buzz and the meds they'd given her, Mary couldn't think straight. On top of it all, the mitered corners of the bed sheet trapped her legs. She kicked until the cotton gave way.

Her injured knee, smothered in crepe bandage, looked more like an alien than part of her body. And Christ, she was going to hurl again. Pain blasted her skull as she reached for the aluminum bowl the nurse had left for her last time she checked her vitals.

Deep breaths. Stress isn't good for babies.

She'd had surgery during the night to repair the damage to her knee, but didn't remember a damn thing since they took her and Tilly away in the ambulance.

Mary wiped her mouth and slid the bowl under the cloth. Out of sight, even so the smell was enough to make her retch. Her head hit the pillow. She'd tried to reach Matt a dozen times during the night, but her real-life hero was off saving the world. She felt ashamed, but right now she wanted him here, holding her hand as she signed the release papers, and got the hell out of this bed.

Mary reached for a tissue. A head bobbed round the open door a second before a tall guy dressed in a crisp blue suit, flanked by her surgeon and two uniformed officers entered her room. "Tilly. I want to see her." Pushing on her hands, she lifted herself higher in the bed.

Earlier they'd assured her the girl and her gran were being looked after, but she had to see for herself.

"The girl and her gran are doing fine. For their safety, we are keeping them under surveillance twenty-four, seven."

Too exhausted to insist, she released the pressure on her hands and sank onto the pillow. "You were at Tilly's house."

"Yes. I'm FBI Agent Todd Rayburn." The suit flashed his badge.

She wished he'd come closer, so she didn't have to squint at the tiny lettering, but maintaining the small distance made her feel less vulnerable.

The doc checked her pulse while the suit reached for a chair. By the way he leaned back and crossed one leg over the other, feigning casualness, Mary guessed what he had to say couldn't be good.

She tugged her hospital gown down over her legs as far as it stretched and lifted her chin. Matt, she needed to talk to him now, but her cell, and I.D., come to think of it, were missing.

The nurse assured her she would check with the team who brought her in for them, but as soon as this guy left, Mary planned on demanding any phone to call him. "What do you want?" She glared at the police officers standing sentry by the door. "I already gave the police my statement."

The doc gave her hand a gentle squeeze and laid it on the sheet.

"Ms. Mary Lane?" Rayburn's voice rumbled next to her.

He must know the answer. "Yes." Her voice was croaky from the anesthetic.

"Ms. Lane. We need to talk."

Her stomach clenched. Rayburn sounded like the cop who came to her house years ago after... *No. Don't go there.* "Like I said, I gave my statement."

"Yes. Thank you. We have a complicated situation." He moved closer to the bed.

Mary cringed and shuffled her backside as far from him as she dared without falling off the bed. His tone sounded forced, wrong, and if her head stopped pounding, she'd tell him why.

"Alexander Volkov, the man behind yesterday's incident, isn't only a kidnapper." Rayburn uncrossed and recrossed his legs.

He isn't only a kidnapper. The words sent a chill down her spine. My organization alerted you to his operation months ago. As soon as we discovered the connection between Tilly's father and Vokov's operation, we've reported regularly how he's targeting vulnerable teenagers in the area where Tilly lives. As we hadn't had any updates, we didn't think anyone listened."

The Agent's eyebrows arched at her tone, and the doc went to check her pulse again. Glaring at him, she closed fingers into a fist.

"As I'm sure you are aware, your intervention and your eyewitness account are crucial in bringing down Vokov's entire operation. The drugs, trafficking. Murder. By now, information concerning his brother's death, your involvement, will have reached him. You are in extreme danger, Ms. Lane."

Mary's hand moved to her abdomen. "What are you saying, Agent Rayburn?"

His expression softened. "We want you to testify at Vokov's trial. Until then, we must ensure your safety. We're recommending you enter the Witness Security Program, WITSEC. Immediately. The officers outside will take you to a safe house as soon as the doctor discharges you." He rose to his feet and buttoned the middle button of his jacket.

"WITSEC? Are you crazy? No. I'm pregnant." Thanks to the pounding in her ears, her words were only just audible.

"I understand this is a lot to process, Ms. Lane, but Vokov and his associates won't hesitate to eliminate any threat to their operation. Your testimony will save countless girls, teenagers. We're close to apprehending him. Until he is convicted, we can protect you and your child."

"Matt?" She felt cold, her skin clammy.

"Your husband?"

"What, no. He's my fiancé. How long?" *Where is my damn phone?*

"Until the trial. Three months at most."

Tears welled in her eyes. "Do I have a choice?"

"Officially, yes. However. Tilly and others like her need you, Ms. Lane." Rayburn's gaze skimmed her body. "Now you're involved and Vokov knows who you are. Your unborn child, everyone you care about, is at risk. His crime network is vast, and the man is ruthless."

The implication that she had somehow caused Tilly's attack made Mary flinch. Closing her eyes, she took a deep breath. Rayburn was right. She had to do this.

Three months. She'd be back before the baby was born. Sure, Matt would be worried, but she'd explain everything to him in a few months. If he was here, things might be different, but he wasn't, and their baby came first.

Assuming she'd agreed, the agent droned on, outlining the process. Mary closed her eyes and stroked her belly. *It's okay, sweetheart.* She thought of Tilly and countless others like her at risk. "I'll do it," she said, her voice stronger than she felt.

"Wise choice, Mary." She despised the veiled threat in his voice. "You'll leave tonight. No contact with anyone—family, friends, coworkers. As far as the world is concerned, Eleanor Lane will cease to exist."

She raised an eyebrow.

"For now," Rayburn added. "If the doc says you're good to go, give these officers a list of essentials and they will pick them up from your apartment." He flipped his chin at the two men who had said nothing.

The doc held his breath for a second, and she hoped he meant to come to her rescue and insist she stay.

"I'll arrange for Ms. Lane's discharge. That knee will need follow up treatment. In the meantime, I'll make sure you have pain killers to take with you."

Chapter Three

"Hey. Where are you going? Beers are on me. That's an order." Bradshaw, Trigger's Commanding Officer flicked his head sideways at the door to the local Sports Bar. He cocked his head to the side, expecting him to walk his ass inside. Stat.

"Permission to take leave, sir." He winked and gave him a mock salute. Bradshaw stared at him. Refusing booze after a completed mission, in his head, equated to fucking insanity.

"On what grounds, Lieutenant?" Bradshaw grumbled.

"Stuff to do, sir." Trig clicked his heels.

"At ease, smartass. It's been real, soldier," he drawled.

His C. O. was the only one on the team who knew this was his last mission, his final tour.

"Remember, if civilian life don't suit, you know where to find us." Bradshaw pulled him in for an unexpected man hug.

Drawing in a breath, thankful he didn't have to use the speech he rehearsed on the plane trip back from Kabul, Trigger watched Bradshaw disappear inside the bar. *Let the party begin.*

A part of him felt like a coward not joining his team and saying a proper goodbye. This was his last chance to hang with men who had had his back through hell over the past couple of years. Strange knowing he may never see them again, but he had a plane to catch and his woman to keep between the sheets for a week.

Discharge papers were signed, and Sentinel had offered him a job in New York. A chance for him and Mary to start that life together they'd been planning. And he better get his ass in gear if he intended to make it home for her birthday, like he promised.

He had plans. Trig chuckled and hailed a passing cab. A surprise dinner with candles and shit. She loved that stuff. Luckily, his bud recommended a place. First, he needed to pick up flowers.

Until he met Mary, Maud Lane, birthdays, Christmas, Easter was nothing to shout about. Pull down the blinds, grab a long neck from the refrigerator, and watch the game. No parties. No cake. No candles. No fucking family.

Mary started hinting three months before her special day, as she called it. The upside. Awesome sex went hand in glove with cake and whipped cream.

Not that he required any excuse to take care of his princess. Pleasuring his woman any which way had kept him sane during long nights in Afghanistan, waiting for the enemy to poke its head out from beneath whatever rock it had crawled under.

She deserved a hell of a lot more than the kiss she insisted was all she wanted to make any moment in her life perfect. Before he left to come home, he'd emailed her, told her to take the day off work, spend it at the spa, pampering herself 'til he got there and took over the responsibility.

His girl was amazing. As well as her day job, she'd been sorting through their apartment, getting it ready to be packed up and shipped to Manhattan. Personal stuff they planned on taking with them in his truck. He was sure as hell looking forward to spending a week together, exploring the Big A, before he started with Sentinel.

Too many hours later, Trig scratched the stubble on his chin and stared at the buckets of flowers inside Morning Glory. According to social media, the best darn florist in Boston.

Behind the counter, the cheery strawberry blonde leaned over the counter and smiled at him. Judging by the way she flashed him a look at her impressive cleavage, she was up for the kind of fun he used to enjoy.

Not anymore. His fiancé, *gee, that sounded right*. The woman with a heart as big as the planet, with a thing for birthdays, owned him. She wore his ring, and he planned on marrying her asap.

"Good evening, soldier. Can I help you?"

"Evening, ma'am. The biggest bunch of flowers you got for my girl's birthday."

"No problem. Anything particular in mind?" The blonde's smile drooped as she swung her curvy ass to the back of the shop.

"No, ma'am. I'll leave it to your expertise." Women had secret intel on this stuff. His feet wore a hole in the floor while she wrangled a giant bow round a bunch of blooms Mary would fucking adore.

"Done. Your girl will love them," the florist winked.

"Thanks, ma'am. Enjoy your evening."

"I will. And thank you for your service."

Outside, he avoided the skateboarder weaving along the sidewalk and hailed another cab. The guy didn't look like he wanted conversation, which suited him fine. It had been a long seventy-two hours.

He ought to call her. Nah, let her wonder if he was going to make it. That way, she'd be even more pleased when he showed. The cab driver pulled up and nodded at the meter. Trig paid, grabbed his gear from the trunk and grinned at the rain landing on the flower petals. Yep, Mary was gonna love them, and he better get inside before they were a bunch of soggy stems.

The doorman, standing under the awning, raised his eyebrows at the pale pink paper covering the bouquet. "Good evening, sir. Good to see you home."

"Evening. Great to be here. Catch you later," he said and headed inside the building.

Standing by the elevator, it struck him that he'd lived in the building for two years and didn't know the doorman's name. Odd, seeing as he was often the first person he saw when he got home, and he appreciated knowing the human guard dog watched out for Mary while he was away.

But, today, hanging in the lobby did nothing to settle the butterflies playing havoc with his gut. A few years ago, the idea of missing a woman, her silky, soft skin, the cute wriggle of her hips as he licked every inch of her, had never entered his head.

His team would call him weird if they knew he had taken a small bottle of Mary's favorite shampoo with him on missions. The smell of lavender and oranges reminding him of how good it felt to bury his nose in her curls kept him motivated.

Trig needed his woman in his arms, right the hell now and this elevator was taking too damn long to get there. He pinched his shirt and sniffed. *Shower first, bud.* Then he'd take his girl on the best date ever. Start at the Rusty Nail. Slip the biggest bowl of duck fat fries in front of her and watch her nose crinkle before she claimed one look at them, slathered in aioli and parmesan, added ten pounds to her ass.

A mighty fine ass, in his opinion. But she didn't have to worry. Mary burned a ton of calories chasing her caseload round town. Often forgetting to fucking eat.

Trig pushed open the door to the stairs and took them two at a time. Outside their apartment, flowers in one hand, he placed his duffle beside him and fumbled in his pocket for the key.

Music played from the neighbor's place opposite. Joan, the odd-ball cat lady with an obsession for hard rock. He chuckled.

No light flickering under the door. Mary ought to have been home hours ago, but then she also enjoyed sitting in the dark with only a burning candle to keep her company.

Thinking on it, he should have called as soon as he landed at Logan, told her he was taking a cab. How many times had she told him she wasn't psychic? Except when it came to him, she was. And he loved it—adored her. She must know he'd be make it for her birthday, realize every goddam bone in his body ached to have her in his arms.

"Mary, sweetheart. I'm home." He picked up his bag, eased the door open and toed it shut with his boot. His hand trembled as he laid the flowers on the kitchen island. "Mary?" His gut twisted.

Too fucking quiet. No hint of his full-of-life lover. If his woman was still at work writing damn reports instead of out celebrating with friends, drinking those strawberry mojitos she loved, she was in for a birthday spanking.

At the possibility, his cock nudged the zipper of his pants. It happened the first time right before he left on this latest tour. No complaints from either of them. He smiled, remembering how her creamy white skin matched the color of the blush on her cheeks.

Trig filled the jug by the sink for the flowers. He'd take that shower, then go find his girl. The apartment lit up as he flicked on the lights as he went. To avoid scaring her, he called out one last time before entering the bedroom, "Sweetheart, you here?"

The first thing he saw was the empty closed. His stomach lurched. A forest of wire and wood hangers, where Mary's colorful dresses and flowery tops should be, taking up more than half the space, scared the ever-loving shit out of him.

Trig yanked open the dresser drawers. A fat load of nothing. A rush of emotion he had no idea how to handle bombarded his chest. Sitting beside the mirror was the blue velvet box. He knew what he'd find before he opened it. *Fuck.* Nestled inside, gleaming against the white satin, was Mary's engagement ring.

"This is not happening", he shouted and slammed his fist into the wall. They had a wedding to plan. Trig pulled out his phone and hit Mary's speed dial, praying he'd hear her laugh. Tell him that diamonds didn't go with her birthday outfit or some such shit.

Hi, this is Mary. I can't take your call right now, but please leave a message and I'll get back to you as soon as I can.

His stomach flipped at the sound of her recorded message. "Mary. Where are you? What the hell is going on? Call me back." His voice cracked. Raw, desperate. Diamonds went with fucking everything.

Running his hand through his hair, he tugged hard on the short strands, hoping the bite would wake him from this damn nightmare. They were getting married. He'd quit his unit for her. Taken the job at Sentinel.

A new life, they'd agreed. Mary had kissed him goodbye at the airport, said she loved him. To hurry home, safe. The nature of their work meant he had to be ready to go wheels up at a moment's notice, but watching her smile, as she held back tears, he was damn certain he loved her and that leaving the military was the best decision of his life.

Jesus. His knees buckled. He sank onto the bed where they should be making love. Wrapped in each other's arms, the light from the street streaking through the window.

They had a future planned. Sure, when he said he didn't want kids, Mary was extra quiet for a couple of days, but she cheered up when he swore after worshipping her every second for the rest of his days, he'd have nothing left to share.

He stared at the folded piece of paper on the nightstand he'd seen when he walked into the room. Telling himself it was the address of her party, he handled it, as if it were on fire, and read her message.

Trig, I'm so sorry. I can't explain, but I have to go. Please don't try to find me. I love you. Mary.

"Hell, no," he roared, crumpling the paper and tossing it at the wall. "What the fuck!" No explanation. No warning. Somewhere rattling around in his bones. He fucking knew. Trust no one. Tears rolled over his cheeks as he read and reread the words.

"Dammit, Mary. What have you done?" No way was she packing her bags and walking out on him without explanation. People didn't vanish for no reason. *What did I do?* Whatever—he'd fix it.

Surging to his feet, he swiped the ring box off the table and shoved it into his pocket. Two long strides and he was out the door. If the birthday girl wanted to end this, she'd do it to his goddam face.

As he thundered down the stairs, a cold sweat broke out under his collar. What if she was in trouble? The protector inside cataloged the possibilities. Each more terrifying than the last. It made no goddam sense. Mary understood what he was capable of, that he'd tear down the planet to keep her safe.

As he burst onto the street, cool night air slapped him full in the face, stopping him dead in his tracks. Whatever was going on in that pretty head of hers, he'd get to the bottom of it and bring her home. He had no choice. Because a life without Mary wasn't worth taking another breath.

Chapter Four

Six Years Later

MARY STOOD ON THE balcony, watching the sun play hopscotch through the trees. Every day, she came to this spot at the back of the apartment, sipped a glass of wine to help her unwind and switch gears before Frank brought Lucy home from day care.

The US Marshal had been there for them since the beginning. Lucy thought the world of him, and she couldn't imagine him not being part of their lives. A token of normal life to cling to at night when she lay awake torturing herself. Thinking of Matt.

The man she would never stop loving. Afraid she'd forget what he looked like, the sound of his voice, she evened out her breath and closed her eyes. It had become a daily ritual, wondering where he was, what he was doing?

A few years ago, she'd asked Frank if he knew anything. He confirmed he'd left the military and worked for an elite security company in New York. Thinking of how easily his life went on without her, she'd cried for days.

Had he married? Did someone prettier, more convincing, made him change his mind, and he had one, two kids? A chill ran over her skin. The possibility made her jealous.

Worse. In her gut, had she suspected when the FBI told her they would catch Vokov, that she'd be back to her life within six months, had to be wishful thinking.

Happy birthday. Mary raised her glass, skolled the last of the red, and listened to the rain assaulting the roof. Six years to the day, and the human trafficker was detained and awaiting his trial date.

Taking a step toward the railing, she opened her eyes and peered into the puddles flooding the flowerbeds. Never too close to the edge, in case she gave into temptation and jumped.

If it weren't for Lucy, she'd have done just that a long time ago. Instead, at least a hundred times a day, she told her daughter how much she loved her. Clutching the handrail, she swayed back into the shadows.

They had no friends in the neighborhood, and she worked from home doing a job she loathed. Data analysis for an online mail order business. WITSEC drove loneliness to a whole new level.

Her parents were dead, and she hadn't spoken to her sister, Sara, in years, long before she disappeared. Not after she sided with their parents when Mary spoke up and told them what Uncle Jack had done to her. No one believed her. Said if it was true, she must have led him on.

The hurt and anger never went away. She should go inside and make Lucy a snack. She'd be home soon, dishing out cuddles, eager to share her day, and hanging outside in the rain feeling sorry for herself didn't get those pop tarts on the table. She walked inside and slid the balcony door shut.

Damn birthday. With the heel of her hand, she scrubbed the tears from her cheek. *Goddam it. There should have been another way.* But Matt had been out of the country, and there had been no way to contact him other than the note she asked the officers to leave.

The clouds parted enough for the sun to highlight the sheen on her daughter's curls as she ran toward her. Blue-black, like her dad's. "Hi, sweetie. Did you have a good day?" Mary swept her daughter into her arms.

"I'm hungry. mommy."

"Okay. Pop tarts? Is Frank with you?" He usually stayed for a cup of coffee.

"No. He's gone."

Scooping the soft bundle of all things good into her arms, she carried Lucy to the tiny kitchen and took the box off the shelf.

"Mommy. Can we have pancakes?"

"It's only Friday." Pancakes were a weekend treat.

"Please."

Mary was a goner even before she added the bottom lip roll. To hell with it. Their life was full of rules. The sky wouldn't fall if they broke this one. "Sure, sweetie." She placed Lucy on her feet. "Go change, while I make them."

The loud knock on the door made her jump. No one came by unless they were expected. Plus, during the first few weeks in WIT-SEC, Frank insisted they treat every knock on the door as a potential threat.

"Grab Floppy Hop, sweetie, and go play our game." Grabbing Lucy's hand, she ushered her to the bedroom. The game was code for, squeeze into the small space behind the bookcase with her favorite soft toy. She adored the soft, fluffy rabbit Frank had given her.

Another loud knock made her stomach roll. "Quiet, sweetie. In you go." She blew her a kiss and closed the door.

"Ms. Lane. Open up. It's FBI Agent Rayburn, Mary."

Her heart skipped a beat. *Damn*, he deserved a black eye for scaring her. What the hell was he doing here? He hadn't been near them in months. She opened the door, not expecting to see Frank standing next to him.

The urge to slam the door in their faces was strong. Nothing good ever came out of Rayburn's mouth. "Come in. I was about to make coffee." Mary glanced at Frank, but he seemed more interested in the knocker on the door than her face. "How do you take it Agent Rayburn?" *Arsenic on the side?*

"Leave the coffee, Mary. Let's sit."

Mary did as Frank asked. "Okay. Spill. What's up?"

Rayburn frowned. "I'm afraid there's no easy way to say this. We got word this morning that Vokov has escaped custody."

"Impossible," Mary snorted. "You're telling me the joint efforts of the FBI and the US Marshals Office can't keep one man behind bars?

A deafening silence answered her question. "When?" Sweat trick-led down her spine.

"Last night. The detail assigned to transfer him to the holding cells at the court was ambushed.

"How?"

"That's not important." Frank said.

To hell it wasn't. His grim expression confirmed her worst fears. "How?" she repeated, trying with no luck to stop trembling. Fight-ing to control the rising panic shuddering through her, she bit her tongue and searched Frank's face for any sign Rayburn was mistak-en.

"We're working on it," he replied. "But we need to move you and Lucy." His eyes darted to the bedroom.

Oh, God. Before he could say another goddam word, she was out of her chair and fetching her daughter from behind the bookcase.

"Mommy," Lucy sobbed.

"It's okay, sweetie." She carried her into the living room. Right now, she was a breath away from slapping the Marshal who'd been an evil necessity for the past six years. Not a friend, more a disease she'd learned to live with. "No. I won't run again."

"Ms. Lane, I strongly suggest you do as the Marshal says."

She remembered the day Frank stopped calling her Ms. Lane. He held her hand when Lucy decided she'd had enough of being cooped up inside mom's belly and pushed her way into the world. "No. I'm sorry. We can't keep living like this. I've followed every damn protocol, changed my name, every part of me, until I'm not sure who the hell I am anymore. Vokov can't know where we are. Right?"

Frank wiggled his chin and loosened his tie.

"Ms. Lane. Unfortunately, we can't be sure. The important thing now is—"

She raised her hand. "The important thing is figuring out who gave me up. Because someone must have, right?

Frank's jaw stopped its wormy wiggle and clenched. She'd struck a nerve. Her mind flipped through every interaction over the past few weeks as Vokov's trial drew closer, searching for where she slipped up, but deep down, she knew the leak hadn't come from her.

"How many people in your office have access to my information?" She pressed, watching for any sign they knew more than they were telling. "I want you both to leave. Now, Frank."

Christ, when she had the flu, this man had made Lucy's bottles, changed her diapers, been there when she took her first steps. "I'll handle this my way."

The system had screwed with her life for too long. If they were to survive, it was time to do what she should have six years ago. Get help from the one person she'd deserted—the man guaranteed to slam the door in her face.

Chapter Five

"Another?" The bartender hovered the bottle over Trig's glass.

"Why not?" He had nowhere important to be. They'd been back three weeks from their last mission. A trek into the Darien Gap to rescue the do-gooder wife of an uber-wealthy kidnapped in South American. If she had asked his opinion before she left, his vote would have gone to Imelda Marcus. *Save yourself the grief, lady. Stay home. Buy shoes.*

It was supposed to be a boy's night out, but his Sentinel brothers had bailed early. Home to their women. Trig tilted his glass. A silent nod to staying single. No one knew how close he'd come to beating them all to the altar or that today was Mary's birthday.

Time he shifted his ass off the barstool. Head home to kick back with a bottle of Jack and watch the ball game. Quiet compared to the ruckus at the other end of the bar.

Should he step in and ask the drunk to remove his hand from Jody's ass? A backside he'd enjoyed touching himself last weekend, by invitation. No woman should have to put up with an unwanted grope.

But Jody could handle herself. He went back to counting the bottles on the shelves in front of him. Shit, he was bored. Needed to get back into the action before he lost his mind. He'd cycled the laundry so many times, his shirts had faded. His go bag sat by the door like a dog waiting for a bone, itching to play with the bad guys as soon as Snake gave the order. *Any day now.*

And that right there was his signal to leave. Forget the game and get some shuteye, except every night, from the moment the moon seized daylight's position in the sky, his argument with sleep began.

"On the tab, Trig?" the bartender asked as he finally made it to his feet.

"Sure."

"Bad day?" Jody asked.

His cock twitched at her sexy, husky voice. One of her best attributes, along with a rack that made his mouth water. Looking like the cat who scored the cream, she draped her arm around his shoulder and dipped low enough to give him an eyeful of stunning cleavage.

"Day's turning out fine." He shifted his gaze to the end of the bar where the guy with wandering hands was talking to his friends. "You?"

The bartender chuckled and spun the towel in the beer glass. Thunder rolled over the roof, rattling the glasses hanging on pegs above the bar.

"All the better for seeing you, handsome," Jody drawled, and kissed his cheek. Yep, time to bail, leave his truck in the lot, and walk home. Psych himself up for another, kill the will to live, day shopping for groceries.

He should have sold that truck years ago. Except Mary loved that Ford Maverick. Named it Beastie Boy, before it cruised out of the yard. That night they'd christened the back seat, screaming his name as his cock drove into her. "You about done?"

Jody stared at him. His one-night rule was no secret. "With work. What time do you finish?"

"Er, I'm ready to go. Right, Pete?" She tossed her dishtowel over the bar.

"Sure. I'll lock up. Enjoy your night."

"Hungry? Wanna get a burger?" He didn't much feel like eating alone.

"No thanks. Not hungry. For food."

The lash flutter was overkill, but Jody had gorgeous hazel eyes. Which he should not have stopped to admire because, fuck him, if they didn't magically turn blue just to annoy him. *Mary, darlin'. Stay the hell away from my love life.* He knocked back the last of his drink and slammed the glass on the counter. "Grab your coat, let's go."

He wanted to wipe the smirk off the bartender's face until he realized he didn't give a crap. Yeah, he was breaking his goddam rule. Hard times called for tough choices.

"My car's the blue Civic. Want me to drive?" she asked.

"Great." At six-foot-three, his legs considered her vehicle a fucking sardine can.

There was a hell of a gale blowing outside, so he offered Jody his arm. Mary loved the wind, used to go for walks at Revere Beach.

Jody slung her bag on the back seat of her Civic and climbed in. Trig folded himself into the passenger side.

"Good to go." She chuckled.

They were a mile out from his place when his phone rang. "Yeah."

"You home yet?" Storm asked.

"What are you, my mother?"

"Hey. Just asking. I'll pick you up at five for PT.

"Can't fucking wait," he growled, forgetting they were starting back at workouts tomorrow.

"Stay safe, bud."

Jeez. Been a dad to Tom, had turned his friend into everyone's parent. He grinned, glad to see him happy. "Later, pop." He pocketed his phone and leaned in for a kiss before Jody started the engine.

Stay safe, had been Mary's last words to him when he left on a mission. And he made sure of it. Itching for the day he returned and took her to bed. Kept her there until they risked starving to death if they didn't shower and eat.

But that was then, sweetheart. Before Sentinel, before her note loaded with the fat, fuck you.

"Where did you go, big boy?"

Jody switched off the engine and straddled him. A freaking acrobatic move in this car. He nuzzled her neck, reached for the lever, and leaned his seat back.

Partee. Happy birthday, Mary. Trig closed his eyes and willed his dick to swell.

***

Zero-four-hundred hours and Trigger lay in bed, nursing his chin. For an itty-bitty thing, Jody had a slugger swing. *Should have stuck to the rule.* No woman slept in his goddam bed. He must have had more to drink than he realized. Plus, he admired her mind blowingly creative skills at keeping his dick awake.

Mary didn't have Jody's experience, at least not when they were together. Six years on, who knew? She was a quick learner. Six years ago, her shy smile had him ready to combust.

"Not cool, Trig. Don't bother calling me. I'm not coming back."

Jody's parting words echoed over the slam of the metal door. *Roger that.* Not cool, whispering another woman's name when you were buried balls deep in the beauty underneath you. Frankly, he was fresh out of give a fucks. He'd turned into the jerk everyone loved to hate.

Five foot six of swinging ponytail, and curves that made his mouth water, dogged every step of his goddam day. Mary had never set foot in his loft, but she sure as hell haunted the walls.

Fuck her. You wish, buddy. Lady-the-hell-Lane dropped her dear loser note on his bed and vanished. At least Jody had the guts to look him in the eye. Make up sex crossed his mind, but she deserved better.

His phone buzzed on the nightstand. He wiggled his jaw and reached for it.

Snake: It's late. Get your arse into Sentinel. Now.

No exclamation mark required. Cloaked in the boss' strong Brit accent, written words were a command. Not looking forward to the PT session, he circled his ankles a few times as a token warm-up, jack-knifed out of bed and saw stars. Woah. Today called for a little less bourbon and a lot more Berocca.

The sooner Knight, Sentinel's founder, signed the paperwork on their new space, the better. The company he'd started in the U.K. was one of the fastest growing, most respected, non-government security agencies, and Trig was proud to be asked to lead the team in their new location.

Leaving his Alpha Team brothers, men he'd lived and been prepared to die beside for six years, would be tough. But he needed a distraction. A fresh start. At celibacy for one thing. He chuckled.

In the meantime, there must be something he could do to escape the city for a few weeks. Maybe he'd ask Snake to send him to help out Beta team. They were up to their necks in Mali. His elite skill set, along with speaking French, had to be a plus.

***

Chapter Six

Mary gathered Lucy out of the car. It was dark. The porch light must be broken, or Sara had forgotten to switch it on for them. Pressing Lucy's head to her chest with her chin, she peered over her head. Careful not to trip, she made her way round to the trunk and grabbed Lucy's bag. A sudden zap of lightning made her jump.

"Mommy," Lucy seized her coat collar. "I don't like the noise." Her bottom lip trembled.

"Me, either, sweetie." Thunderstorms had always scared the crap out of her. She nuzzled her nose against her daughter's neck and couldn't resist a quick sniff of her sweet smell. A miracle after the long car trip. She badly needed a shower that would have to wait a while longer.

"That tickles, mommy." Lucy giggled.

Since Frank told them Vokov had escaped, there hadn't been time for any fun. The play times she loved as much as her child. With a whoop, Lucy's pudgy fingers tugged on one of the gold teardrop hoops from Matt had given her as an engagement present. Today, she wore them, hoping they'd bring them some much needed good luck.

"How about we leave mommy's ear where it is, sweetie?" Reaching one hand into her shoulder bag, she pulled out Floppy Hop. "Look who I found." She tickled the bunny's ears under her chin.

"Come on, let's get you inside." Hitching Lucy higher onto her hip, she pressed into the wind, threatening to topple them over. Standing in Sara's driveway, it crossed her mind, not for the first time, that she shouldn't have come. Her earlier phone call with Sara had been tense.

More lightning strobed across the sky, illuminating Lucy's small face. Like Matt, she had brown eyes. One look at them and her heart melted.

"Mommy, I'm scared."

Gently, she lowered the thumb from her daughter's mouth, gave it a quick kiss, and hurried up the porch stairs. "It's okay, sweetheart. We'll be inside soon." *If your aunt opens the door.*

Matt had been with her the last time she was here. They laughed hard and long when her stuck up sister complained about how much noise they'd made during the night. Ordered them to have more respect. Of course, Matt saw it as a personal challenge to make her scream louder the next time they made love. He enjoyed getting under Sara's skin, and Mary never stopped him.

Desperate to get inside before they froze to death, she knocked loudly on the door. "Sara."

The door opened a crack, and her sister peered at them, disapproval etched into her frown.

"Jesus, Mary. Do you know what time it is?"

"Sorry. No control over the weather. The roads are bad." She squared her shoulders and planted half a foot inside the door. "Are you going to let us in or not?" Sara didn't have to do much to draw her into a fight. Some things never changed.

Lucy squirmed, her eyes flicking from her to her grumpy aunt. *Christ, coming here is a mistake.* She shifted her weight to return to her car when the door fully opened.

"Come in. Take your shoes off," Sara grumbled.

"Down, mommy."

As she slid down the front of her body, the tip of Lucy's elbow connected with her nose. *Ouch.* Parking the suitcase by her side, she toed off her boots and helped Lucy with her shoelaces.

Lucy threw her arms around her leg and squeezed. Stiff from the long drive, it ached. "It's okay, baby," she whispered. Taking hold of one hand, she picked up the suitcase with the other and followed Sara to the living room. "I need a favor, Sara." Her voice shook.

"Seriously? That's how you start this conversation? You disappear for six years, no word, until a few hours ago, and you want a favor?"

Had her sister always had such thin lips? Swallowing her pride, she forced herself to answer. "Yes. Sorry. I need you to take care of Lucy. Just for a few days." *Fingers crossed.*

"Why? Where are you running off to this time?"

Ouch. The question hanging in the air was as heavy as the storm clouds overhead.

"Oh, for Christ's sake. Sit down. Both of you." Sara peered down her nose at Lucy. "I'm going to make coffee. When I come back, we'll talk about why you are here.

I wasn't clear?. Mary rolled her eyes.

"You do still drink coffee?"

"Sure. Thanks." Her leg was killing her, and because a part of her childishly remembered the fun of irritating her sister, she tugged on Lucy's hand and sat beside her on the floor. They never sat on the furniture at home. Why start now? "Any chance of a cookie?"

Sara lifted an eyebrow. "I suppose so. When did you last eat?"

"When we stopped for gas," Mary lied. Lucy batted her hand when she tried to unzip her coat. "Okay, sweetheart, leave it on. Give me a hug." She cuddled her daughter and rehearsed possible answers to the million questions coming her way when Sara returned.

The house was enormous, two, maybe three levels, and no sign of anyone else living there. Old family pictures covered the walls. None of her. One of Mitzi, their golden retriever, made her smile. The dog who sat with her when she hid in the tree house at her mom and dad's home and cried.

A few minutes later, hips weaving round the furniture, Sara placed the tray of coffee and a plate of chocolate chip cookies on the small table.

"Wouldn't you be more comfortable sitting on the couch?" Sara accused.

Mary shifted Lucy off her lap. The child's bottom lip trembled. "Come and sit up here with mommy." She dug the heel of her hands into the seat behind her, heaved herself up, and patted the spot beside her.

"Does she need, er, changing?"

Placing her hands in Lucy's armpits, she raised her above her head and sniffed. "Nope. Don't believe she does." Lucy giggled, and she sat the wriggling imp on her knee to prove the point.

"Jesus, you're more of a child than your daughter." Sara huffed.

Fair point. "Sorry, but Lucy is five. Completely toilet trained."

"Fine. Now, tell me why you're here and why you need me to look after your daughter."

Over the next half hour, she shared the highlights of the past years, and enjoyed her sisters' gasps and nods.

"Okay, let me get this straight. You are the star witness in a child trafficking case and the bad guy escaped police custody and is after you. That it?"

"In a nutshell." Mary wanted to slap her. "Forget it." She shifted Lucy onto her feet. "Come on, sweetie. Time to go. Say goodbye to your Aunt Sara," she sneered.

"Oh, sit down, for heaven's sake. You look like you haven't taken a deep breath in years."

She wasn't wrong there.

"If what you say is true."

Mary pinched the thin skin on the back of her hand.

"I don't understand why the marshals can't help you find somewhere to deposit your daughter?"

Her heart pounded. "I'm not putting my kid into care."

"There you go. Running away with a story. I didn't mean it like that."

To hell she didn't.

"Not an institution. Fostering? With people who look after children until their parents are able to take over or..."

"I'd rather she stayed with family." *Family.* Not loving where the conversation was traveling, Mary sprung to her feet. "I have to find Matt."

Sara bristled. "Matt? And how do you think that will work out after you practically ditched him at the altar?"

I had no choice. Facing him may be difficult, but not as terrifying as the alternative. She glanced at their daughter, clutching Floppy Hop. "I have to try, Sara. For Lucy's sake." Her voice cracked. "Please."

Silence stretched between them, broken only by the relentless drumming of the rain.

"Fine. But Mary? When you see Matt, don't be surprised if he wants nothing to do with you. He was a broken man after you left."

Her gut rolled. If only he'd been there that day, instead of off somewhere saving the world, maybe they could have gone into WIT-SEC together.

She'd had to act quickly. Vokov may still have been in the area that night, looking for her. The FBI assured her that he would hurt anyone she cared about, so she chose to hide to protect him and their unborn child.

"Thanks." Before Lucy fully understood what was happening, she made her move. "Everything you need is in her bag. Her bedtime stories are on top. I wrote a list of her favorite foods. Make sure she sleeps with Floppy Hop." Her heart almost broke when a tear trickled down her child's pale cheek.

"It's only for a few days, sweetheart." She fished a tissue from her pocket. "Come on blow. That's my girl. You'll have fun with Aunt Sara."

Whispering promises she wasn't sure she could keep, she hugged Lucy and headed to the front door. The chill running down her spine had nothing to do with the wind. But for her daughter, a chance at a future free from looking over their shoulder, she'd face Matt and whatever else waited for her in Manhattan.

"Be good, sweetheart. I love you."

Lucy nodded, her bottom lip trembling. "Love you, Mommy. I'll be good."

She brushed her lips over her daughter's forehead and walked outside. Sara followed. "Thank you for this. I'll call when I reach the city."

"Wait. You better take these."

Mary frowned. What was her sister offering? Valium? Christ, she might be tempted. Anything to lower the panic simmering under the surface. It took a sec to realize the keys Sara dangled were the spare set to their parent's old house. A house that didn't hold too many happy memories. At least not for her.

The keys were rusty from where they'd spent years living under the rock by the front steps in case either of them got locked out. For Mary, that had been more often than their father liked.

"It's not too far out of Manhattan and it's empty. No one has lived there. Not since..."

Mary nodded. Not since the night their parents died in a light aircraft crash coming home from The Hamptons the first summer after she left home. "Thanks. I'll return them as soon as I can."

"Okay. Call me when you arrive."

"For sure." She kissed Lucy one more time and fled down the stairs to her car.

"Mommy." Lucy screamed and tried to break free from Sara's grasp.

Sobbing, she started the engine and tore down the driveway.

Chapter Seven

Mary pushed open the heavy wooden door. Back-to-back long drives were a serious test on her leg. A dull ache radiated from her knee to her shoulder blades.

She prayed for courage, because that's what it took to enter her parent's house. Two steps inside and she froze. With a howl, the door slammed shut behind her. Before it settled, the beat of the knocker thudded along with her heart. Standing in the hall, nothing looked as though it had changed. A few more cobwebs and, of course, the ghosts.

Sara accused her of making up stories. No need when this place held plenty of true horrors. Turning left into the main room, she ran the tips of her fingers along the row of pink flowers on the arm of the couch. Her favorite place to sit after school and do her homework.

In front of the fire, while her mom and dad were out at a charity event, she and Matt kissed. Their first. Awkward. Perfect. Stretched out on the rug, spooned together, the heat from his body warming her skin through their clothes, they had fallen asleep. Her father woke them and gave them hell.

Mary shaped the thick dust covering the huge oak dining table into the shape of a heart. Along one side, a row of dining chairs faced the windows that looked out on mom's garden. In the morning, she'd check to see if anything had survived.

In the corner of the room was her mother's favorite armchair. A book lay open on the small table next to it. In the evening, she never missed reading a chapter before going to bed. She must have forgotten to take it when they left for their vacation in the Hamptons. Tears clogged her throat.

Damn. She felt sick. Scrambling to the bathroom, she flicked the light switch. Dead. Her heart raced. Vokov? *Steady, Mary. The house has been empty for years.*

Sucking in a calming breath, she looked up at the moonlight filtering through the skylight, highlighting the basin and metal taps. Splashes of icy water on her face soon settled her stomach. She didn't remember the last time she'd had anything to eat or drink, other than candy and coffee.

Less than twelve hours since she left Sara's, and already she missed Lucy so much it hurt. Feeling miserable in her parent's house was not helping. *Close the door on the past, and drive to the motel a mile back.*

Pity she only had sixty bucks in cash. Not enough for a room, and if she used her credit card, she risked Vokov finding her. The walls felt like they were closing in on her. Literally, not knowing which way to turn was driving her nuts.

She had many faults, but indecisiveness wasn't one of them. As a social worker, thinking on her feet had been a strength. *And look where that got you.*

Cursing, she threw a damp, dusty hand towel at the wall and screamed. She should never have left the note at Sentinel asking him to meet her here. The woman who took it bristled when she mentioned she was a friend of Matt's. Apparently, Mary meant some guy called Trigger.

But she had, so there was no finding a motel until then. She didn't have the strength to run from him again. According to her phone, she had half an hour. That's if he showed. Plenty of time to walk back to the roadhouse for a burger. Best not to face him on an empty stomach.

Grabbing her purse, she closed the door behind her and stepped onto the porch. Rain lashed her face. She counted her footsteps splashing through the puddles to stop from letting her thoughts running away with her.

The back of her neck prickled. Ahead, she was sure she saw a man duck behind a tree. Shielding her eyes from the rain, she watched for any movement, too scared to move.

Woah. The ghosts have followed you from the house. Her thin chuckle disappeared into the heat behind her coat collar. With precious seconds lost, making it to the roadhouse and back in time seemed impossible. Forcing her aching leg to keep up with the other, she hurried back to the house.

If she didn't eat tonight, she'd live. The extra weight gained when she was pregnant still clung to her hips. Dying of starvation was the least of her worries.

Start a fire, and figure out what you're going to say if, when Matt arrives. Given he didn't want children, telling him he had a daughter may not be the wisest way to start. But the man she used to know would protect any child with his life. Even if he wanted nothing to do with her.

The creepy sensation running through her body grew as she neared the house. Numb from the cold and fear, she fumbled with the keys. The front door opened a split second before a large, suffocating hand covered her mouth and stifled her scream.

Whirling round, Mary came face-to-face with the man she'd been dreading, longing to see, for the past six years. "Matt," she whispered. Lightning tossed his face in and out of the shadows. Eyes she remembered being the color of melted chocolate, were now cold, black with anger.

***

Fuck! Mary smelled amazing. A hypnotic gut punch that needed to stay the hell out of his life. Trigger clasped her arms behind her and nudged his knee against the back of her thigh. Her neck twisted at an awkward angle as she searched for what hit her.

The light from the street picked up the silver flecks in her pale blue eyes. Four years he searched before he gave up hope of finding her.

He sucked in a breath, but oxygen loved playing hide and seek with his fucking lungs. "Been a long time, babe."

"Too long," Mary gasped.

Her sweet ass pushed against his arousal. Rock hard since he first spotted her, his cock wanted to throw a welcome home party right here on the porch.

Chaining Mary to his bed for a fucking week, for old time's sake, amounted to serious temptation. *Never. Gonna. Happen.* Choices had consequences. Mary had once meant everything. He'd have died for her. Still would.

And what was with the limp? She did her best to hide it, but keeping stuff from each other had never been possible. He relaxed the wrist pressure and felt her shudder ripple through him.

"Matt? Can we go inside?"

"Sure." He toed the door open and nudged her forward. If he was smart, he'd leave, except moving on required answers to a shit ton of whys. Close to the top of his list, why turn up now? What did she want?

"Please. My wrists. You're hurting me."

Payback's a bitch. "Sorry," he snarled, and released her. As soon as she rubbed her forearms, pink from the pressure of his fingers, the temperature in her folks' place dropped ten degrees. Itching to kiss away her pain, he released his grip.

Like he did when he first saw her standing on the other side of the street, he channeled ice through his veins. Visualized an avalanche of snow, burying the desire to drag her into his arms and just fucking hold her.

Determined to hang onto his disintegrating control, he turned his back on her and took inventory of the old place. Someone had tossed one of her mom's handmade quilts over the back of the couch, to hide worn spots, he guessed. For the most part, everything else was untouched.

Behind him, Mary sighed. *Look at her. Not yet.* Trig stepped closer to the credenza lined with family photos. None of her. Fair. She dumped her family, too. With a shrug, he turned.

Still breathtakingly beautiful. Her hair was shorter, and there were thin lines and dark shadows beneath her eyes. "What was his name?"

he asked, brushing her cheek with his palm because he couldn't fucking resist.

"'Scuse me?" Mary stared at him.

He enjoyed the fact she was struggling to make sense of him, shuffling her feet, deciding whether to step out of the doorway and sit.

"Come in, babe." Trig smiled. *That's it, bud. Stay on top.*

Her chin lifted. "Nice of you to offer."

Good to see she hadn't lost her spunk as she waltzed her way the long way round the couch and sat at the far end.

"What was his name? The man you chose over me?" Mary's breasts surged underneath her coat. *Fuck.* He wanted to rip the damn thing off her body and palm her beautiful tits, pinch those nipples until she begged for more. She liked that, at least she did, before she ran. Pain? Regret? Fear? Something flashed across those pretty blue eyes.

"There hasn't been anyone else, Matt." She shoved her hands in her coat pockets and shivered.

His cock pressed against the zipper of his pants, eager to narrow the distance and share some warmth. "Okay, relax. No big deal. Just curious." And behaving like a complete dick. Yeah, well, that's what happened when you ripped a guy's heart out.

"If you need money, you should have sent a text. Now, you're here, let's come to an arrangement," he sneered. He seldom said no to a high-priced fuck with a stunning woman.

Rubbing her wrists, her gaze stayed fixed on him. Before she left him, every inch of her five-five body had been his downfall. Her plush mouth, her hips, breasts. Thighs that gripped like a vice when she came. Her delicate ears were the perfect shape for the tip of his tongue.

He slumped onto the other end of the couch. "Sorry, babe. Need to keep moving. Why are you here?" He should shoot himself in the goddam head for caring.

"I had no choice. I need your help."

And every fiber in his body wanted to yell, hell no. The days of moving heaven and earth for her were over. "Help with what, Mary? Or do I call you something else these days?" He cocked his head to one side. "Mrs. — "She clasped her hands in her lap until her knuckles turned white.

"No, Matt. Last time I checked my birth certificate, "Eleanor Lane is still my name."

"Maud?" She hated her middle name. "Eleanor Maud Lane," he corrected her. "Or did you give your grandmother's name away, too" She raised a perfectly shaped eyebrow and half-smiled.

"Do you remember the time you teased me about my gran's name and my dad overheard you? I thought he...

The words tumbled from her mouth and in a flash, he was grasping her arm. "No, babe," he growled. "Not in the mood for a stroll down fucking memory lane. Tell me how much you need, so I can arrange transfer, and be on my way."

"What? No. Please, listen."

His fingers stayed a fraction too long on her soft, silky skin before he released her. "Places to be, people to see, sunshine. Send me an email." Hell, if he'd hang around for a chat. It only took a couple of keystrokes to deposit funds into her account.

"Matt."

No one had used his first name in a long time. Mary's shoulders sagged. Was she giving up? Letting him leave? His chest tightened. "Okay, you have five minutes, babe."

"Would you like a drink? Whiskey, right?"

Mary rose from the couch. Hyper, unsure. Nothing like the woman he remembered. Her touch, the flutter of her sure fingers over his skin, used to bring him peace. As she walked to her father's liquor cabinet, her gait stuttered. The limp bothered him, but they'd get to that. "Bourbon. I never touch whiskey."

Chapter Eight

Bourbon. How could she forget?

"Forget it, Mary. Clock's ticking. Get to the point. Why are you here?"

The coldness in his tone, until now something she'd never felt from him, seized her breath. *Fine.* If he didn't want to be civil, no reason not to pour herself a drink. God knew she needed it. Aware of him standing behind her, she knocked back a shot and savored the burn.

"Mary?"

"WITSEC. I've been in hiding," she blurted. Matt snorted. He didn't believe her.

"You always were creative, but that's, let's say, whimsical even for you, sweetheart."

Longing for the caress that often accompanied the endearment, she kneeled in front of him and tilted her head. Would he cup her face, like he used to, brush his mouth over the pulse point on her neck? No chance. "It's the truth."

"Okay. I'll bite. Why?"

Her heart thudded. "Sure, you don't want that drink?" She jumped to her feet.

"I'm sure, but if it helps, pour yourself another, then sit. Who the hell have you been living with since you left?"

That hurt. The not-so-subtle implication she'd been sleeping with anyone else, when it was the fear of Vokov knocking on her door that kept her awake at night. *Alone, except for the company of our daughter.* She wanted to scream at him, but why give him the satisfaction of making her lose the control she'd hung onto all this time? "The FBI wanted me to testify. I had no choice. I had to..."

"Save it." Matt cut her off.

He'd been in the military when she met him, and he never spoke much about the long months they were apart fighting for his country, for her. But all that time, the hardness in his eyes, that had never been there.

"Six years, Mary. Without so much as a fucking text."

The muscles in his thighs tensed. "No. Wait. Please." Familiar sparks shot along her arm as her hand fell on his shoulder. "You weren't there, and I..."

Matt brushed her hand away like it was an annoying bug. Her gut clenched. "Sorry. That came out wrong. I don't blame you, but I had to make a quick decision. I chose to protect you, and to keep our..." Desperate for that connection, she skimmed her fingers across the back of his neck. He had to understand.

"Take your hand off me."

Shivers ricocheted along her spine at the quiet harshness of his tone. Far worse than if he'd struck her. "I couldn't risk anyone being hurt. If Vokov had any inkling that you or my family knew where I was..."

He laughed. "This keeps on getting better, babe. Vokov. Great name for the bad guy. Come on, Mary. Protecting me? That's rich. I was an elite paratrooper, for Christ's sake. You didn't know details, but you understood what I was capable of, what I would do to anyone who threatened what was mine."

Lightning flashed outside the window. *Oh, God.* She had caused the pain illuminated on his face, so this time, when he went to stand, she didn't stop him. She didn't deserve his help?

Matt towered over her. She felt small, defeated, but for Lucy's sake she would not give up. "I know. Big, bad Matt Anderson, I should have trusted you."

"I'll set up a meeting. Sentinel will decide whether to take your case. If they do, the boss will assign protection. Dex or Havoc. Two of our top operatives."

"Not you?"

"No. Not me. I won't be in town much longer."

His words hovered like an unexploded grenade. "I understand." Her breath hitched. "But, after what we had...shared, there's something else. We..."

Matt raised his hand. "Had Mary Maud. You got it right the first time. What we *had*."

In case she wanted to push the boundary, she guessed, his voice was low and dangerous. *But if he uses my middle name again, I will stab him in the eye.*

"Whatever we had died the day you stopped trusting me and vanished."

Mary flinched. A part of her aching to hold the only man she'd ever loved in her arms, obliterate the hurt buried in his brown eyes. "I understand. Thank you for coming. I know you must be busy." Not sure what to do next, she sat in the spot he'd just left and closed her eyes.

A waste of time. Until she felt Matt's finger and thumb grip her chin.

"Look at me, Mary."

His warm breath settled on her skin before their lips touched, and his tongue plundered her mouth. Keeping her eyes closed, she prayed dreams came true. Gripping his wrists, she rose to take all he was prepared to give. "I missed you, baby," she murmured, opening her eyes to his colder than hell gaze.

"Yeah, me too." His head cocked to the side. "One more for luck? No. Let's quit while we're ahead." He released her chin and stretched to his full height. "See you again in another six years, babe. Snake, the boss, will be in touch."

"Bastard."

"For sure. A lot has changed. I never took you for a..."

The door slammed shut. "A what?" *Hell, no, you are not walking away.* For Lucy. Dammit, for him. The idiot deserved to know he had a daughter. Dragging herself off the couch, she rushed after him.

"No. You can't leave," she yelled.

Watch me. He didn't need to say the words. They poured from his body as he stalked to the truck parked on the street at the end of the drive. Their truck. Should have upgraded by now. Red hot tears mingled with the rain on her cheeks, the icy water soaking through her thin jacket because hope was devil in her book.

Angry at the dumb son of a bitch, terrified she wouldn't reach him before he drove off, she ran after him. She didn't hear the roar of the bike until it drove alongside her. Matt spun round a split second before a gun fired.

"Mary!"

Heart pounding, she ducked behind her mom's favorite rose bush. Bare from neglect, it offered no cover. Two more shots shattered the front window. A firm hand gripped her arm.

"Come on." Shielding her with his body, Matt half-dragged, half-carried her toward the porch steps. "We're not done talking."

Turning her head over her shoulder, she spotted the biker raise his gun and fire. A bullet whizzed past her ear. "Matt." The rider skidded past the end of the drive, gifting them with the precious seconds to reach the house.

"Get behind the couch and stay the hell down."

Looking every inch the bad ass, he drew a gun from the holster at the back of his jeans and edged along the wall to the broken window.

"Your past has caught up with you, babe." He slipped the edge of the curtain to the side.

"I thought you weren't going to help me." Mary gulped for her next breath.

"Old habits die hard," he muttered.

Five heart stopping minutes later, he returned his gun to its holster.

"Looks like your friend's gone."

Yeah, the man deserved that stab in the eye.

"Start talking. And this time, fill in the parts you left out."

And whose fault was that? Mary hesitated. His bitter insulation earlier that she had left him for another man stung. "No." *What's the point?*

"No?" he repeated, his brow furrowing. "Not a good idea to test me, Mary. Last chance."

She straightened her spine. "You're right. Whatever we had died years ago. Don't trouble yourself setting up that meeting. I've had a hell of a day, and I need sleep."

"Sleep? Some mother fucker just tried to kill you," Matt yelled.

She didn't dare hope there was a hint of concern mixed with obvious frustration. "I'm aware, *babe*, but I've survived this long." Her voice held steady, thank Christ.

"Don't be stupid."

"That's rich." Childish, yes, but she couldn't resist tossing her chin in the air. "You're angry with me. I get it, but if you're done, I'd like to run a bath." Mary watched the struggle playing out on his face—his desire to protect warring with his need to be a million miles away. "I'll contact the Marshals. Providing they're not too pissed off with me, I'm sure they'll find us a new location."

"Mary." Matt's voice rumbled with warning.

"Goodbye, Matt." Before she changed her mind, she opened the front door and swept a path along the hall to the street. "Stay safe."

"Fine. Lock up. Call the police."

Fat lot of good that will do. As the door slammed shut, tears cascaded over her cheeks. Coming to New York was a mistake.

It didn't take long to pack her bag, lock up the house, and throw her belongings into the rental. Vokov would find them. For the second time in her baby's brief life, they had to disappear.

Chapter Nine

"Fuck! Fuck! Fuck!" Trigger pounded the steering wheel. Pain shooting from his wrist to his elbow. Damn woman shredded his insides. Like he promised, he'd been sitting in his truck, about to call Snake, when he heard the roar of the motorcycle engine, followed by the sharp crack of gunfire. If Mary hadn't ducked behind that stupid bush, she'd be lying in a pool of blood in her mom's front yard.

Years with the military, then with Sentinel and he'd never been as terrified as when he heard those shots. After grabbing his sidearm from the glove box, he reached her as she was dragging herself off the ground.

His heart took a nose-dive as he skimmed her body, checking for blood, a sign she'd been hit. Mad as hell, he'd behaved like a dickwad.

Not his finest moment, implying she left him for another man. She denied it, and in his gut, he knew it wasn't true, but he pushed until tears killed the fire in her eyes.

Trig scrubbed his forehead. *I haven't slept with anyone else.* Liar, liar, pants the fuck on fire. El had the face of an angel, but she'd never been a saint. Why should she be any different from him? If a trophy existed for sleeping around, he'd be holding that damn thing high.

I missed you. Right. His cock sure missed Mary Maud Lane. And as for the whole WITSEC fairytale. Vokov, Schmuckov? Fuck the hell off. But back there was no random shooting.

Someone wanted Mary dead, and that scared the bejesus out of him. Mud sprayed across the windshield. So, to spite his better judgment and blue balls, he was all in. *God help me.*

The wipers thudded back and forth across the windshield. *Pull over dickwad, before you kill yourself and the driver on your tail.* Trig signaled and ground to a stop at the side of the road. *Damn her.* He let Mary Maud in once and she almost destroyed him. Not going to make the same mistake twice.

After five minutes of allowing the steady rhythm of the wipers to match the jump, tuck, and roll of his heart, he called the boss.

"How did it go?" Snake asked.

The Boss had been there when he read Mary's note asking for the meet. Wasn't hard to tell something was wrong when his knees refused to hold him up. "Just peachy." Sparing the ugly, personal details, he brought him up to speed.

"You still in Connecticut?"

"No. On my way back to the city."

"Anyone call the cops?" Snake asked.

"I didn't." He'd lay money she hadn't.

"Aha."

"And what the fuck does that mean?" That's all he needed, the boss playing parent.

"Shirking responsibility? Not like you, my friend."

"Yeah. Okay." He'd stuck around long enough, debating whether to apologize, to see her leave. "The cops never arrived. She left. I want to know who this fucker is."

"I hear you. She tell you anything more about why she's here?"

"Says she was in WITSEC. Hiding out from someone called Vokov."

Snake's whistle rang in his ear as the wheels of a semi sent a wave of water cascading over his truck. "Boss?"

"Alesandro Vokov?"

"Could be. You know him? Who is he?"

"Pakhan of the Bratva in Boston. A low life shithead. Into child trafficking and drugs. FBI has been after him for years."

"Goddamit. Russian Mafia."

"Right. Your girl got herself mixed up in some heavy stuff.

"She'd not my girl." He bristled.

"If you say so, but Trig, you need to find her before it's too late."

Trig rattled off her plate number. Who knew why he memorized it, but he was mighty glad he had.

"Great. Storm's right here. Give him a sec to track her location."

"Thanks, Boss." Underneath his eye twitched. He must be goddam losing it when waiting two minutes seemed more like a week.

"Okay. Looks like she's heading for Boston. Not far from where you are."

"Thanks. From memory, her sister lives there. I'll check in once I have her."

"Do that. In the meantime, I'll have Hawke dig for the latest on Vokov."

***

Mary sniffed and peered at the road ahead. Since leaving the house, her tears hadn't stopped flowing. She hated it. Feeling sorry for herself took her focus away from what mattered. Getting to Lucy.

Shifting her head toward the open window, she sucked in the chill night air and eased her foot onto the accelerator. Poor visibility, but she drove as fast as she dared.

Streetlights whizzed past at hypnotic intervals. A smart idea would be to pull over, spend the night at a motel, but she had no chance of sleeping, plus Sara's place wasn't much further.

I can't help you. I'll get Snake to call you. Matt, the over-protective man she'd almost married, would never have entrusted her safety to anyone else. Not if he knew she was in danger. How could she have been so wrong about him? Fallen in love with a storybook hero. *Nice job, Mary.*

Keeping one hand on the steering wheel, she fumbled under the papers on the passenger seat for her phone and rang Sara. "Come on, pick up." Like the previous times, the call went to voicemail and her anxiety leap-frogged into the red zone.

A horn blaring startled her. The oncoming truck almost clipped her before she swerved out of its path. Jerks thought they owned the road. Flipping him the bird as he passed, Mary smiled even though her hands were shaking.

If she wanted to reach Sara's in one piece, best pull over at the next opportunity, fill up, and grab a snack. Thankfully, she didn't have to wait long. Only a couple of miles before she parked, grabbed her purse, and hurried into the diner.

As the automatic doors parted, the smell of grease and over-brewed coffee hit her. Sauntering in her direction, a waitress waving a steaming jug filled with black sludge nodded at a booth by the window.

"Coffee?"

"No, thanks."

"Okay, I'll be back in a sec to take your order." She pointed at the menu tucked behind the sugar.

"S'okay. Make it a BLT on rye." Mary shrugged. "Hold the lettuce."

"Sure thing, honey."

Like Matt had taught her, she shuffled along until her back was to the wall and scanned the other diners. Situational Awareness, he called it. Know the enemy before they strike. Huh. He forgot to add that the enemy had cloned the man she once believed was her everything. She bit back her tears. *Not here.*

People equally exhausted from driving in the treacherous weather drank the coffee and waited for their food. What she wouldn't give for a magic wand. The words 'turn to dust' hovered on her lips as she thought of making them disappear. Placing her elbows on the table, she cradled her chin, willing herself not to fall asleep.

When the doors groaned open, heads turned to stare at the six-foot-four, incredibly well-built man enter. *Damn him.* Her eyes locked on Matt. Regret, concern, and something else she was afraid to name hardened his features.

The rugged mass of power and strength strode toward the booth with the assured grace and confidence of a panther about to pounce and devour its prey. Reaching for the glass of water in front of her, she sipped and ignored him. Waited for the bomb to drop.

At the same time she turned to look out the window, a man standing outside raised his rifle. The waitress saw him too, screamed and dropped the plates she'd been carrying. *Not again.*

"What the fuck?"

She heard one of the other customers shout as Matt lunged for her, tackling her off her seat and under the table as another shot shattered the window.

"Hell. We gotta stop meeting like this, babe." Matt grinned.

The man was insane. Pinned under his weight, the heat of his body consumed her, cradled her in the peace she'd given up thinking she'd feel again. The sensation was short lived. Vokov had found her.

***

Matt slammed Mary to the ground and shielded her with his body. Allowing anger to cloud his judgement, leaving her at the house unprotected, could get her killed. And this woman attracted gunfire like flies to the honey cakes she loved. He shook his head. *Dumb time to remember shit like that, Trig.*

Sirens wailed in the distance. Scrambling for cover, panicked diners picked their way through shattered glass. Mary trembled beneath him. "Are you hurt?" He'd landed hard on top of her. She was small, half his weight, but a bruised rib or two beat a fucking bullet to the chest.

He stroked the strand of hair away from the side of her mouth, gutted by the shock reflected in her wide eyes.

"I... I don't think so."

She winced and squirmed underneath him. "Your leg?" One hand on his weapon, eyes peeled, Trig eased onto his elbow. "Better?"

"All good."

Not true. As soon emergency services showed up, he'd make sure the medics checked her out. On cue, Massachusetts's finest swarmed the café. Trig stayed low until they'd finished their sweep before rising to his feet.

"Stand up." Trig reached for her hand and helped her to a seat away from the window. "Hang on a sec." He slipped his arm around her waist to steady her and brushed the broken glass onto the floor. "Okay, sit."

"Thank you. Matt, I..."

He placed his palm on her trembling knees. "Shh. Where were you going? Never mind. Doesn't matter." He huffed out a breath. "You're coming with me to Manhattan." The words surprised him. Kind of. Not. Hell, he wanted to kill.

"Manhattan? Why? I thought you didn't want to help me."

"Clearly, I was wrong." Doing his best not to lose it, he ran a hand through his hair. "Be smart, Mary. Don't argue. If Vokov found you here, he can find you anywhere. Sentinel has resources, contacts."

"No. I don't need your help." Her eyes darted to her ringing purse.

"Answer it." *Her husband?* Why wasn't he here taking care of her?

"No."

Her spine straightened, the way it did when he ruffled her feathers. "I'll call them back. Thanks for the offer, Matt, but I can't go with you. Vokov will come after you and your friends?"

Mary's hand rested on his, and for the space of an inhale, he almost caved. "Let him. Sentinel has a safe place big enough for the guy calling you to stay, too."

Her brow furrowed. What? She didn't trust him to act like a grown-up and play nice? He'd give it a shot.

"Okay, but..."

Trig shrugged. "Hey. No one's forcing you, babe. Say the word and I'll arrange for someone to take you wherever you want to go."

"Matt, please. Don't do this. I've said I'll go with you."

"Fine." Taking a deep breath, he faced the cop walking toward them. "We'll leave as soon as these guys finish questioning us." Unable to look her in the eye in case she saw the relief pouring off him, he tossed the words over his shoulder.

Taking Mary's elbow, he intended to meet the cop halfway when her eyelids fluttered, and the color drained from her cheeks. Trig scooped her into his arms.

"Put me down."

"Not happening. I suggest you lean into me and suffer unless you want your ass to hit the ground." Her sigh swept through him, tugging on parts of his anatomy he'd rather stayed sleeping. "Relax," he muttered as much to himself as her. One thing for sure, he didn't care who joined her in Manhattan. Mary was under his protection until Vokov died.

Chapter Ten

Vokov paced the length of the luxurious penthouse, his polished shoes clicking against the marble floor. He turned his head and gazed out at the Manhattan skyline. At night, the glittering horizon calmed him, along with counting backwards from one hundred in his native Russian.

The routine stopped him from slitting throats or putting a bullet in the back of someone's head. He chuckled. Simply because he was in a bad mood. He enjoyed playing the cliché villain, complete with maniacal tendencies that oozed D C Comic intensity?

The moon hadn't shown its face yet, still hidden behind the stormy clouds. Somewhere out there, the American bitch who killed Maxim was alive. His brother would never forgive him if he let his death pass unavenged.

"Another drink?" his lover asked. His dark silhouette mirrored in the window.

Not too close. The man had learned when to give him space. Vokov waved his hand and kept his eyes on the cloud drifting across his horizon. His hand clenched his empty glass. The darkness in his mood hadn't lifted since his first vodka. No reason to assume a second would do different.

"You're sure, *dorogoy*." His lover pressed.

"*Da*." He waved off the man who shared his bed, but little else in his life. Although, more recently he'd ensured his escape from custody.

"We will find her." The man raised his glass, already celebrating the win. "It's only a matter of time."

His lover's kiss no longer burned with the fire it used to. Vokov put down his glass before it shattered in his hand. "Time?" he spat the word "*Moy brat*, lies cold in the ground and Mary Lane still breathes. Every moment the bitch lives is an insult to Maxim's memory."

The silence stretching between them took too long. He shouldn't be here. He should be out there, vowing not to return until Mary Lane and her brat were found. He contemplated shooting him, but Maxim would object. Always the voice of reason. His councilor.

"*Dorogoy*, maybe you should let this go. You're free. Let's focus on getting out of the country. Starting a new life."

"Let. It. Go?" Vokov spat out the words, moved with lightning speed, and grabbed the idiot by the collar. He slammed him against the glass shelf, embedding his knee against his cock. Leaning closer, he bit his lip until drops of blood stained the front of his white shirt. "My brother is dead because of that bitch. Are you seriously asking me to walk away, forget his murder?" His lover flinched.

"I'm asking you to survive." He brushed his tongue over his lip. "The feds won't stop looking for you. Every day we stay in New York we are at risk. We have contacts in South America, new identities ready for us to step into and disappear."

Disgusted, Vokov shoved him aside. "I will not leave. Not while she and her daughter live."

"And what happens after you kill them? Is revenge worth throwing away our chance at a life together?"

The fool asked so he told him. "My life ended the day Maxim died. All that's left is to make sure she pays." By the look on his face, the man who had once been as close to him as Maxim, did not appreciate his answer.

Vokov walked to the wall safe and unlocked it "I don't care how long it takes. I don't care what it costs." He took out several five-hun-dred-dollar packs and waved them in his lover's face. "Find Mary

Lane and her daughter. Take pleasure in watching the light leave their eyes when I shoot them."

"*Dorogoy*."

He saw red at the note of warning in his lover's voice.

"Using a child as bait. That's crossing a line."

"The line was crossed when she murdered Maxim. Are you with me, or not?"

"Always *Dorogoy*." His face settled into a resigned mask.

"Good," Vokov returned to the window. The city stretched out before him, a hunting ground, and his prey couldn't hide forever. He raised a silent toast to his lover's retreating back. "Soon, Maxim", he whispered. "She will pay for what she did."

Chapter Eleven

Pinpricks of light ran across her vision, and the headache from hell pounded in her head. That didn't mean she enjoyed being swept off her feet in front of everyone.

Much? Mary. She had been close to passing out. Matt carried her effortlessly. The beating of his heart resonated all the way to her toes. And he smelled wonderful. A familiar blend of musk and citrus guaranteed to make her horny as hell.

Allowing herself to believe being in his arms meant anything special bordered on masochistic. The elite warrior turned body-guard was programmed to help anyone in trouble. "Put me down, Matt." Not much of a stand, seeing as they'd reached his truck.

"As you wish."

He held her tight, their bodies close, as he lowered her toes to the ground. Reaching behind her, he opened the door. Hot all over, she didn't appreciate the cocky grin on his face.

"Up you go."

As though she weighed no more than Lucy, he planted his large hands on her hips and lifted her into her seat. Matt had always been fit, but the man had developed muscles on muscles since she'd last seen him. Pity his brain hadn't kept pace with the growth rate.

To stop from fanning her flushed cheeks, she clasped hands together in her lap and tried to ignore the tingle rippling across her pelvis.

Neither of them spoke. They had always been comfortable in each other's company. No words necessary. But this was different. One look at the scowl on his face, and nobody would believe he had a great sense of humor. Never failed to make her laugh when the glums chased her. *Forget it. Stop torturing yourself.*

Mary shuffled deeper into her seat. As soon as they got wherever they were going, she'd try Sara again. Let her know what was happening. Matt's hand drifted in her direction and for a spine-tingling moment, she hoped he'd give her thigh a reassuring squeeze. She needed it.

When his fingers settled for turning up the heat, she bit her tongue in case she begged. Clearing her throat, she turned to face him. His steely profile gave nothing away. "Okay, if we make a stop? I need to use the bathroom."

"No. It's late. I want to get to the city. Need my beauty sleep, babe. If you need a distraction." *Mind reader.* "There's a Hershey bar in there." He waved at the glove box as if she was a cranky kid cranky with a long road trip.

His sweet tooth was legendary. A miracle he still had teeth. "No thanks. I'll wait."

"Suit yourself."

Confused, unsure if she'd made the right decision coming with him, she leaned back and closed her eyes. Shutting him out offered protection against the heavy mood inside his truck. Maybe she should have said thanks, but no thanks, hopped in her car, and pressed on to Boston?

No. She had made the right decision. Keeping Vokov as far away from Lucy was her priority. She gnawed the end of her thumb.

"We're here."

Matt's grumble dragged her back to reality.

"This is Winter's home. One of Sentinel's top operators and a man I trust with my life. He and his wife, Maggie, are waiting for you. You'll be safe with them until Sentinel figures out what to do with you."

"How did they know I was coming?" Her skin bristled at the idea of being dumped.

"Called while you were sleeping."

His tone reminded her of her dad when he thought she was being dim. How she'd love to tell him to stick a Return to Sender label on her forehead and she'd be on her way. Forget the fairy tale. The story where they went to his place and had six years of monkey, make-up sex. *You're pathetic.*

And pissed off. Time to tell him about Lucy, his daughter. "We need to talk. You..." her voice quivered.

"Don't," Matt cut her off, his gaze meeting hers. "Just... don't."

"Really. You have no idea what I'm going to say."

"Whatever it is. I don't want to hear it."

His flat tone riled her even more. "You are an idiot. I didn't ask you to follow me to my parents' house. Didn't plan to be shot at in broad daylight." Her voice hitched.

For a brief second, she swore his gaze softened before his eyes turned stone-cold black. *Oh, yeah, go to hell coming right at ya.* Except the man was out of the truck, grabbing her bag and marching up the stairs of the brownstone before her addled brain formed the sentence and marching up the stairs.

Standing on the sidewalk, she admired the way his butt cheeks clenched. There had to be some perks in this hell. Been tackled to the ground earlier had aggravated her knee. Stiff and sore, she tried not to hitch her hip as she climbed after him.

Matt shook her bag. "Maggie's about your size. I'm sure she has stuff to lend you until there's a chance to shop."

"No. I'm fine. Sounds like they are doing enough to help a stranger. I can't ask her to lend me..."

With a shrug, he banged on the door.

Asshole. Cutting her off combined with his one-word answers drove her crazy. As a father, he needed to grow up. *Christ.* When she told him, what if he didn't believe her? And there was still the problem of him never wanting children in the first place.

Her mom's voice, claiming Mary did anything to get attention, echoed in her head. After she had explained what happened with her uncle, her entire family accused her of being a liar.

Ready, steady... She closed the space between them. Matt deserved to know the truth. The door swung open.

"There you are. Come in, come in. It's freezing out there."

The warm smile on the pretty red head's face faltered. Maggie, she guessed, sensed the tension between the two people on her doorstep.

"Er, hi, Trig. And you must be Mary. I'm Maggie."

"Hi." Matt thrust her bag into Maggie's arms, forcing her to take a step back. "Sorry. I've got to go. Tell Winter I'll check in with him later."

It was the early hours of the morning, and neither of them had slept. Where was he going? Without so much as a catch-ya-later, the jerk headed down the steps as if his ass were on fire. Dumbfounded, she watched him pull out his phone and stride to his truck, leaving her feeling as worthwhile as the bag sitting like a gigantic teddy bear in Maggie's arms.

Lowering it to her side, she ushered her inside. "Come on in, Mary. Let's get you settled."

She hesitated long enough for Maggie to step closer and curl her free arm around her waist.

"Look, I know this isn't ideal, but you're safe with Winter and me, and from what I gather from my husband's cryptic comments about your situation, that's the important thing. I won't pry." She nodded at Matt's truck. "But if you want to talk, I'm here."

Mary nodded and faced the open door. "Cryptic?" she asked. Did Matt tell everyone his long-lost fiancé had returned? Maggie didn't answer. *What is it with these people?* Fine, the idiot pulling away from the curb had an excuse for giving her a hard time, but... "You're being rude," she blurted. The redhead stopped dead, and her arm dropped to her side.

"Sorry. Did you say something? Heck. Winter will be mad as hell when he finds out I haven't got my hearing aid in."

"Oh. I didn't know. You're..."

"Deaf. Mostly. No big deal. I also read people's lips, but that means I need to look at them." She laughed.

Inside the brownstone, they were halfway up a flight of stairs when a man met them coming the other way. His eyes lit up as soon as he saw his wife. Matt used to look at her that way, like there was no one else in the universe.

His hand reached for the bag she was still carrying. A few years older than Maggie, Winter was as tall as Matt, the same, seen more than he should in life, lines etched into his weathered skin.

"Hey, sweetheart. Let me take that. Where's Trig?"

"Birdbrain left. Said he'd catch you later."

Mary laughed at Maggie's eye roll. Boy, it felt good. As if for the first time in years, she may have an ally.

"The hell he did."

The scowl on Winter's face disappeared at his wife's gentle headshake. Mary wanted to reassure them it was for the best, that she didn't care, but somehow in the past forty-eight hours her tongue had tied itself into a gigantic knot.

Winter pushed open the door to a bedroom. The pale, gray-blue tones of the walls and furnishings had an instant calming effect.

"Hope you'll be comfortable here, Mary. Holler if you need anything." He kissed Maggie's cheek. "See you soon, sweetheart. Gotta head into the office for an hour."

"No problem."

After the front door clicked shut, Maggie ushered her into the guest room.

"So, how do you know Trigger?" she asked.

Mary tensed, unsure how much she wanted to share. "We were... we used to hang out together," she answered. "It's complicated."

"I understand. Trigger is a great guy, but he's, er, intense."

"I'll say."

Maggie glanced at the clock on the shelf. A pink rabbit with ears that waved in sync with the ticking. "I know it's early, but are you hungry? Do you like tea? Jenna, Storm's wife, has me hooked. She's English." She winked.

"Not hungry, but I'd love some tea before I crash."

"Awesome. Follow me."

And like they'd known each other for years, Maggie giggled and swooped her in for a hug.

Downstairs, in the kitchen, waiting for the jug to boil, Maggie pulled a opened a container full of brownies. "I made these earlier. Do you like chocolate?"

Mary's stomach sounded like a volcano getting ready to blow.

"I'll take that as a yes." Maggie smiled and placed the pot of tea, cups with saucers, and tiny plates with pink rosebuds on them on the table. "Enjoy."

Grabbing the one closest to her, she sank her teeth into the sugary temptation. "Oh my god," she mumbled around the mouthful. "These are incredible!"

"Good. Experiment a success. I'll take some into Sentinel later for the guys to munch on." Maggie beamed and poured the tea.

Chapter Twelve

Storm and Winter flanked him as they strode into Sentinel's War Room. The room where Snake briefed them on their latest missions, and the team worked out a strategic plan of attack.

He'd slept a few hours in the back office before Winter caught up with him and chewed him out for leaving Mary the way he had. What did he want from him? Mary was safe. That was the main thing. The only thing that concerned him.

Winter's home might look like a typical Brooklyn brownstone, but it was a fucking fortress, even before Maggie became his reason to live. Recent modifications made it stronger than Fort Knox. He needed time to get his head on straight and claw back the control he'd lost.

"Come on, give. What's with you two? You've been giving each other the hairy eyeball ever since I got here." Storm slapped him on the back.

Fuck me. "Nothing man. Leave it."

"Hey." Palms up, his teammate took a seat and crossed his arms over his chest.

Jeez. That was some pout. Trigger remained standing close to the exit while Winter sat next to their friend.

Trig assumed the boss had called this meeting to discuss Mary and her situation. Winter knew now, but eventually, he'd have to let the rest of his team know their whole, sad as fuck story.

It surprised him to see Knight sitting with Snake at the head of the long table, huddled over a laptop. Trig struggled to make out what they were saying over the tapping of their rapid keystrokes.

Sentinel's head honcho didn't honor them with his presence often. As the company's founder, and a doting father, the grumpy alpha dog preferred to command international ops from their main headquarters in London.

Knight had established connections in power corridors many never knew existed. Rumored to have a direct line to the President of the United States of America. How he'd swung that was a mystery.

Was he here to complete the paperwork on Sentinel's new office? Hell, he hoped so. The move to Arkansas, taking on the new challenge, couldn't come soon enough.

With a heavy sigh, he pushed off the wall and lowered his body into the empty seat across the table from Storm and Winter. Outside, the light glared bright yellow off the windows of the building opposite.

Trig shuffled the papers in front of him. The quicker they worked out a security detail for Mary and tracked down this Vokov shithead, the sooner he could start packing.

"Patience, brother." The toe of Winter's boot connected with his under the table.

Storm squinted at him, but he was in no mood for a guilt trip.

"Digging into WITSEC files isn't a walk in the park," Winter added.

"What the fuck?" Storm groaned.

"Understood," Trig shot Winter a chin lift, stopping short of pointing out the Sentinel brochure stated, Elite investigators. *What the hell was taking them so long?*

Knight, the imposing, flicked his head side to side. The loud crack focused everyone's attention, including the woman staring down at them from the big screen at the other end of the table.

"Hawke pull up Mary's WITSEC dossier," Knight ordered, looking straight at him.

"Mary? Who the hell is...?" Storm asked.

"Zip it." Winter answered.

Knight sighed and turned to Snake. "How about you, me and Trigger take this into your office?"

He sprang to his feet, sweat cascading down the back of his neck. The time for giving a shit what his teammates might think about him and Mary was over. "No. Nothing to hide. Spit it out."

Snake ran a hand through his hair. "Your call, Trig."

You got that fucking right.

"Sit down." Knight nodded at his chair.

"I'll stand, thanks."

Knight turned to face the overhead screen. "Thanks to Hawke, we now know why your fiancé was in WITSEC."

The room tilted. Trig sat before his ass hit the floor. Mary had told him the truth.

"Fiancé?" Storm gulped.

"Shut the fuck up." The collective command sang from the group.

"Ex fiancé," he clarified. No point in anyone getting over excited. He fixed his gaze on Storm.

Snake hit a key on the laptop and another report flashed onto the screen. "See for yourself. It's all here. When Mary witnessed the attempted kidnapping of a girl on her caseload, she walked into a world of pain. An international human trafficking operation run by Vokov. Russian mafia. Talk about being in the wrong place at the wrong time. Word is he's calling in any and every favor. Won't stop until he finds your, er, Mary."

Hell, he was having a fucking heart attack. Trig leaned forward and scanned the screen. "Vokov," he muttered. *What the hell, Mary?* Social workers were frumpy do gooders, though she never owned that, who fed the homeless and wrangled services for people without. They didn't play with human traffickers.

He thumped the desk and cursed. This intel changed nothing. Back then, Mary hadn't trusted him to help her, so why start now? Any of his Sentinel brothers were more than capable of protecting her. "Okay. Assign someone to her and I'll pay the tab. For now, she's safe at Winter's. Firm up a security detail and I can leave for Arkansas. That's if I still have the job?" His knees trembled under the table.

"You got the job, arsehole."

Knight made it sounded more like an insult than congratulations.

"Okay. Everyone, take a big, fucking breath. Trig, there's more," Snake said.

"Don't need the set of steak knives, boss." Trig joked, his eyes glued to the screen. Guaranteed, he was going to hate the next thing that came out of the boss' mouth. The click of the mouse button ricocheted off the walls like a weapon being cocked.

The face of a cute kid looking down on them was a gut punch.

Storm gasped first, mainly because Trig couldn't breathe. He was right. Mary had been a busy girl.

"Hell, she's cute. Congratulations, man." Storm gushed.

"Not mine." He shrugged. Trust his best friend to get it wrong.

"Records show she is five years old. Name on her birth certificate is yours, Trig."

No fucking way. "Not possible," he stated. The dipshit father must have dumped them, and she pulled his name out of the hat.

"You okay, man?" Snake asked, his voice laced with concern.

"Not sure." At least, that was the truth. "If she was mine, Mary would have told me. Why keep it a secret?" Married or not, he'd have taken care of them.

"C'mon, Trig. You know WITSEC protocols are strict. No contact. Break the rules and the door closes. You're on your own."

Too many emotions warred inside him to put up with Snake's condescending tone. "Fuck that. She should have come to me." Betrayal, anger, and a fierce protectiveness coursed through his veins. He eyeballed Snake and Winter, defying them to take her side.

Knight slammed the laptop shut. "I suggest you get your shit together and go talk to Mary. Find out for sure if you and the kid share DNA. Bring Mary here when you're done. In the meantime, Hawke will gather more intel, then we will work on the next steps for keeping them safe."

In the fog surrounding him, people were talking, but the eyes of the girl on the screen followed him as he walked to the door. The kid wasn't his. Mary knew he didn't want children.

"Hey bud. I'll drive. You call Maggie. Tell her we're on our way."

Winter's hand on his shoulder pulled him out of his downward spiral. Storm fell in step beside them. No point arguing. He was in no fit state to get behind the wheel. Plus, they might be able to stop him from putting his hands around Mary's pretty neck and strangling her.

Chapter Thirteen

THE LATE MORNING SUN streamed through the upstairs window, casting long shadows over the wide floorboards. Fresh and free of unwanted dust and animal hair. A huge step up from the worn, stained carpet in the safe house that never smelled or felt clean, no matter how often she vacuumed.

From the first day Frank handed her the keys, the place gave her the shivers. Knowing she wouldn't have to stay there long had kept her positive. Reality hit the day Lucy came into her world. They weren't going home anytime soon.

Yes, they caught Vokov, but Frank insisted if they wanted to stay safe, they must stay in the program until after his trial and conviction. But technicalities and adjournments meant the date kept getting pushed back further.

Days morphed into weeks, then months. As the years slipped by, it broke her heart and ultimately her spirit. There was no going back to what she and Matt had shared.

Curled up in the guest bed, her sleepy thoughts slipped to their last night together before he left on his last tour. Over pizza, they'd made plans for their married life in New York. A fresh start. Although that future became fiction, remembering them had helped keep her sane during the long nights sleeping alone.

A huge yawn stretched through her entire body. She wasn't sure how long she'd slept, but she needed a shower. Swinging her legs over the edge of the bed, she took a couple of deep breaths and let her knee adjust to the idea of taking weight.

The room oozed with feminine touches. The giant teddy bear propped in the chair in the corner, wearing a gorgeous pink knitted hat. The way the buttons popped on his hair chest. All Maggie. The bear's big brown eyes begged to be hugged. Lucy would love him. Her chest tightened, and a lump the size of Mount Rushmore rose to the back of her throat.

Reaching for her phone, she called Sara, who still wasn't picking up. *Answer me.* She let it ring a few more times before tossing the phone on the bed and moving to the bathroom.

What if Vokov had found Lucy, or there'd been an accident? Her sister wasn't the best driver, and if the weather was as bad in Boston as Manhattan. Tears welled in her eyes. Her body ached to hear Lucy's laugh.

When she couldn't get the faucet to turn, Mary stared at her trembling fingers and cursed herself for leaving Lucy. When the phone rang in the other room, she almost tripped in her rush to answer it. "Hello."

"Mary?"

Sara's clipped tone rang with familiar accusation. "Yes." *You called me.* "Is Lucy okay?"

Sara huffed. By the time her sister spoke, she was ready to poke her eyes out. It wasn't enough that she wasn't there. Sis enjoyed making her suffer.

"She's fine. For now. But Mary, you need to be here. Your daughter needs her mom."

Mary closed her eyes and counted to ten. "I know, I know. I'm sorry, but I had to try."

"Hmph. How did it go with Matt? Will he help you?"

She clenched her fist, her nails dug crescent moons into her palm. "Let's say he wasn't exactly happy to see me."

"I warned you. Walking back into his life like you haven't been missing for years and expecting to pick up where you left off. Did you tell him about Lucy?"

Sarcasm and frustration. The go-to approach whenever her family spoke to her. "No. I'm waiting for the right moment."

"Jesus," Sara hissed. "There is no right moment. What are you going to do? You there, chasing your ex- fiancé, Lucy, here. It's not fair. Did you think your visit was going to be full of sunshine and rainbows?

Would have been nice.

"It's not always about you. I have a niece, but I don't know her. I have work, friends. A life."

The implication she had none of the above hurt.

"I can't stay home babysitting, afraid to leave my home again because of the danger you parked at my door." Sara droned.

Mary's breath roared in her ears. *Danger? Doorstep.* "What do you mean? Has something happened?" Another long sigh. Her phone felt like it weighed a ton.

"I think we're being watched."

"What? Why?"

"Yesterday, we were both tired of being cooped up, so we went for a walk in the park. There's one nearby. Of course, I haven't spent much time there, but we found the play area and..."

"Sara. Please. What happened?" Mary screeched. Hell, the walls were closing in on her. Clutching Maggie's bear to her chest, she sank onto the bed.

"I'm sorry, but maybe if you were here..."

"Sara!"

"Lucy was playing on the roundabout with another boy, and there was this creepy looking guy started talking to her. At first, I thought he must be the other kid's dad."

Mary clasped her throat. "Christ, Sara. What did you do?"

"I went over to see what was going on, of course, but as soon as he saw me coming, he walked away."

"Don't leave the house until I get there. I'm leaving now." But she didn't want to risk using her credit card by hiring a car. "I can't risk using my credit card. I'll have to take the train and pay cash."

"Okay. But hurry. Or..."

"You'll what?" Behind her, she heard footsteps a second before Maggie stepped into her room. "My sister." Mary hung up and wiggled her phone.

"What's going on?" Maggie asked, one eyebrow raised at the bear in her other hand.

Embarrassed, she set it down on the bed and gave its tummy a pat. "Sorry. I have to leave." And if Maggie hoped blocking the doorway would stop her, she was mistaken. If she had to, Mary would knock her over and apologizing later.

"Oh, no. Trigger will have a fit, and Winter will tan my backside so hard I won't be able to sit for a week." She smiled. "Come to think of it, that might not be so bad."

"I have no choice. I have a daughter, Lucy. She needs me. My sister saw a man talking to her at the playground. The man who is after me must have sent him. She's in danger." The words spilled out of her. She had to leave right now before the maniac destroyed the one person she loved more than anything in the world. I'm pretty sure there's a train in the next hour.

"Okay. We'll make it if traffic cooperates. Let me call Winter. If this son-of-a-bitch is making moves on your daughter, he and Trig will..."

Her breath came in short bursts as she made a dash for the door. "Sorry, I can't wait." Pushing past her, Mary rushed down the stairs and out the front door. A gust of wind almost knocked her over.

"Okay, okay, I'll drive you to Penn Station." Maggie hollered.

Mary blinked, stunned by the offer. "You'll help me? What about Winter?"

Maggie nodded. "I'll deal with him, but nothing is going to happen to you on my watch." She half smiled. "But don't say I didn't warn you. When the guys find out, they will go ballistic."

Heart pounding, Mary returned Maggie's weak smile. "I'll tell them I snuck out and stole your car.

"Yeah. Hubster won't believe that for a second. Wait, while I fetch my keys and my..."

Maggie pointed to her ears and ran back for the aids while Mary waited in the doorway. The rain roared like a beast, and the damp seeped into her injured knee.

Maggie reappeared with an umbrella. "Okay, let's go." She aimed the fob at her car. "Ready?"

At the sound of the beep, they huddled together, made it down the stairs, and slid inside the red Honda Civic. A shudder ran through her when Maggie turned the key, and nothing happened.

"Hang on. Brian can be temperamental."

When it still didn't start, her heart sank. "Is it the battery?"

"It shouldn't be. Winter checks everything." She slammed her palms against the steering wheel. "Okay. We can't sit here."

On that, they agreed. Calling an Uber or a taxi wasn't an option. This time of day, they'd wait too long. Mary knew what was coming next as soon as Maggie swung to face her.

"I know you said no, but we have no choice. Let me call Winter."

"No. He will tell Matt, and I can't deal with him right now. He's made it damn clear he wants to be as far away from me as possible."

"Oh, honey."

Maggie squeezed her hand. "I can't wait any longer. Thanks for trying, I'll take the subway. Which way?"

Maggie sighed. "Fine. I'm coming with you."

"Christ, I could kiss you."

"Later. Come on." Maggie locked the car and hooked her arm through hers.

Wind whipping across her cheek, Mary limped beside her as they hurried the couple of blocks to the station. She was about to ask Maggie to slow down when they reached the entrance. And the stairs. Grabbing the handrail, Mary turned sideways to start her descent to the platforms.

"I don't like this," Maggie muttered.

"It's fine," Mary assured her, even as her insides twisted. Cool, damp air whistled through her clothes, chilling her to the bone, as she paid for her ticket, and turned to say goodbye to her friend. She held out her arms for a hug. "It's okay. I'll be fine from here. Thank you."

"No way. I'm coming with you to Penn, and I'm not leaving until I see that Amtrak train pull out of the station."

"Thanks." It felt good not to be alone.

"And the minute you get to Boston." Maggie paid for her ticket. "You call me, and every two hours after that. And before we go any further. Is Trig, Lucy's father?"

Wow. Caught off guard, Mary nodded.

"Okay. Add telling Trig to the list." Maggie nudged her elbow.

"Will do." She didn't have to know the last thing Matt wanted was a kid crowding his style.

Standing on the subway platform, the press of bodies and stale air did nothing to calm her frayed nerves. She looked around for a seat, but they were taken. A woman walked past them, pushing a small trolley loaded with shopping bags. How had she got it this far?

Ten minutes later, as the yellow lights of the train emerged from the tunnel, Mary felt a violent shove from behind. Time slowed to a crawl as she teetered on the edge of the platform, arms pinwheeling, hands clutching at air.

"Mary!" Maggie screamed.

Twisting her body, she threw herself sideways. With brutal force, her knee slammed into the concrete as the train passed and stopped. Hands came from everywhere, dragging her to a seat.

"Oh my God, Mary. You're bleeding."

Maggie's pale face swam into view. Searching for a glimpse of who pushed her, she searched the crowd.

"I'm calling Winter," Maggie said firmly, pulling out her phone. "We need to get you out of here."

Her stomach rolled and the edges of her vision blurred. *Shit.* "I need air."

"Okay. Hang onto me."

With her friend's arm wrapped around her waist, they made it out of the subway and onto the sidewalk. Sheltering under the Expressway, she took a large breath and regretted it. The blinding pain shooting through her ribs numbed her brain to anything Maggie had said.

She was too busy keeping her breath shallow to register how long they stayed huddled together, trying to stay dry, before Winter's SUV pulled up alongside them and he leaped out.

"Are you okay?" He cupped his wife's cheeks.

"Yes, hon. I'm fine."

Winter turned to face her. "Come on. Let's get you out of here."

Pain was doing strange things to her head, like screwing with time. One minute she was having trouble standing, the next she was in the back seat of the car, Maggie sitting beside her. "Damn. Did I pass out?"

"Only for a few seconds." Maggie squeezed her hand. "Trigger's waiting for you at the house."

Her stomach clenched. "He is? Why?" Winter's eyes met hers in the rearview mirror.

"He'll explain. For now, relax."

"Put your head on my shoulder." Maggie offered.

"Thank you. It wasn't Maggie's fault. I made her come with me," she blurted, anxious to keep her new friend out of trouble.

Winter said nothing until they arrived at his brownstone. "Hang on, Trig will help you out." He nodded at the steps.

Matt was halfway down them. His black T-shirt wore his body like a second skin. Furious, judging by the grim look on his face.

Maggie beat her out of the SUV and met him at the bottom of the steps. "Hi Trig, we didn't expect to see you here."

Jeez. She loved this woman.

Chapter Fourteen

TRIG SIDESTEPPED MAGGIE. TRUST the youngest member of their tight Sentinel family, if you didn't count the growing number of his teammates' babies, to call out his bullshit.

He bent to open Mary's door and narrowly avoided a mouthful of metal. The woman was quick to make it clear she needed no help. He shifted, giving her space to pass, and waited until she finished hobbling up the steps before he followed.

She didn't do a half bad job of hiding her damn limp, but the dark circles under her eyes, her ashen skin? Shit, out of luck there. Mary was in pain, and he was fast losing patience with her refusing help.

Placing an arm around her waist and the other under her thighs, he swept her into his arms and carried her inside the house. She weighed one-hundred-and-ten pounds max, less than the pack he wore in the field.

Feeling her soft curves rubbing against him as they walked made his cock stand up and take notice. And damn, she felt like home. Pity they were stuck in a place called never again.

Circling the coffee table, he sat her at the end of the couch. Frustrated by the temptation to reach for Maggie's knitted shawl and wrap it around her trembling shoulders, he came out fighting. "What the hell happened? You were supposed to stay put and out of trouble."

"Hey, don't yell at her. Someone tried to push her in front of a train. That's what happened," Maggie roared.

"Easy, sweetheart." Winter pulled her close.

Trig sniffed in a breath. Around Mary, he did that a lot, searching for fucking oxygen. "And that, damn it, is why you shouldn't have left this house." He drove his fist into his palm.

Mary recoiled as if he'd slapped her.

"Cool it, bro'." Winter shifted forward.

Trig shook his head. "Back off." The guy knew he would never lay a finger on her.

"I can't stay here. My sister needs me." She struggled to stand.

Trigger cursed and grabbed her arm. "Sit down." He nudged her back onto the couch. "Please," he added, lowering his voice.

"Let's go grab a coffee and give these two love birds some space, sweetheart. They have shit to discuss."

His friend slipped his palm to the center of his wife's lower back and gave her a nudge.

"An apology is a great place to start." Maggie squinted at him.

For a shortstop, the fiery redhead was damn fierce. Trig had a hard time holding onto his smile as she marched up to him.

"You know where the first aid kit is. Take care of her before you let Rambo off the leash." She kissed Mary's cheek. "I won't be far away. Call if you need me."

"Will do. Thanks. For Everything."

The light glistened off the tear in Mary's eye and he almost lost it completely.

"Any time," Maggie said, placing another kiss on Mary's other cheek.

As he closed the door on his friends, he prayed he'd keep it together long enough to hear what his ex had to say about the kid. He returned to where he'd left her.

"I'm sorry."

She grabbed his hand, the pad of her thumb brushing across the back inside of his forearm.

He wrenched free, but despite ordering his dumbass body to keep its distance, he dropped to his knees beside her and ran his palm over her thigh. Well-toned muscles bunched under his fingers.

"Oh, Matt."

"Don't worry, honey. Strictly medicinal. Call it due diligence. You're limping."

"Oh. I'm fine. I came down hard on the platform. Bruised my ribs. Few scratches. Should be healed in a few days."

"Good to hear." He gave her an A for the brave face. "In the meantime, I'll fetch that first aid kit. I'm sure Maggie has a mirror. You can bathe and take care of the cuts on your face while I finish my book."

"Fine."

The way her eyes turned from sky blue to inky sapphire when she was mad at him had his cock remembering the good 'ole days. "Like hell you will. Back in two minutes. In the meantime, before you vomit over my friend's furniture, do me a favor, lay back, and rest.

Get your shit under control. Never in his life had he failed to keep his emotions in check, but Mary pushed every one of his goddam buttons. Curling his fingers around the edge of the bathroom sink, he splashed cold water on his face. After filling a bowl he found in the cupboard with hot water, he grabbed the first aid kit. He left the goddam mirror. Small steps.

Trig's heart skipped a beat. Mary lay on the couch, head slumped to the side, eyes closed, her chest rising and falling with her breath. *Aw, sweetheart. What the fuck happened to you?* Sure, Vokov wasn't someone you wanted to get mixed up with, but the father of her kid must have been a heartless coward to leave her on her own.

Fuck, no. His gut somersaulted. *Vokov?* If that mother fucker had violated her, he'd kill him twice.

Trig placed the water and kit on the floor beside the couch and picked up her delicate wrist. Pulse steady. A second morphed into three, then a whole minute as he tried to let go of the soft beat of her heart under his fingertips.

"Mmm. Sorry, I didn't mean to nod off." Mary stared at their joined hands.

No, siree. No way. Not going to lip smack the woman who'd walked away. "Close your eyes. I'll clean those cuts."

"You don't have to. I can do…"

"Not this, again, babe. Playing the martyr gets old real quick." He laced the words with the command she used to respond to. As competent and independent as she most certainly was, she loved him to lead. Back then, her trust had made him feel ten feet tall, King of the Universe. Until it didn't.

"Matt, I..."

"No one calls me that anymore. Trigger or Trig will do fine." He showed her the tip of the damp cloth and waited for her nod before gently pressing it to her cheek. Red and angry, the scratches had to be sore, but she didn't so much as wince.

"I see. Thanks, Trig." She rolled her eyes. "Boy, that sounds weird."

And it did, coming from her mouth. *You'll always be her, Matt.* "Yeah, well. Things change." He dabbed the cuts dry with clean gauze. "Start at the beginning, Mary, and tell me what happened."

"Sara called, said I had to come quickly. Maggie offered me a lift to Penn Station, but when the car didn't start, we headed for the subway."

Still no mention of the kid. "Go on. Get to the part where the asshole with numbered days attacked you." Her face turned paler than pale. *Believe it. Dead man walking.*

"I remember feeling pressure against my back and then the next thing I'm trying not to get creamed by the oncoming train."

Trigger cursed, fear swimming through his insides.

"Somehow I landed on the platform."

"Jesus, Mary."

"I'm sorry, okay. I should never have come with you to Manhattan, but..." her gaze dropped to the hands clasped in her lap.

"Look at me, dammit. But what?" Trig growled. Something you needed to mention before you took off again. Everything, Mary. From the beginning."

She flinched at his tone. "Trig, I..."

"Stop. You have no idea what it did to me when you left? And now you're asking for my help and keeping secrets. You're fucking unbelievable." Hands on his hips, he paced in front of her.

Tears welled in her eyes. "I never wanted to hurt you." With a sudden move, she swung her legs off the couch.

"Yeah, well, that ship sailed."

Mary drew in a shaky breath. "We...have a daughter."

Trig froze, along with the words hanging in the air between them. "No" he whispered.

"She's five, and a bit, if you ask her. Her name is Lucy."

For the first time, Mary smiled, a genuine light up his fucking world smile. His hand twitched, desperate to kiss her senseless.

"I left her in Boston with Sara. That's why she's calling me."

His whole body trembled with a mix of shock, anger, and goddam pain. *Five. And a bit.* The rush of emotion almost brought him to his knees.

"I'm sorry. I should have told you sooner."

"You think?" Trig folded his arms, staving off the itch to wring her neck. He didn't have it in him to hurt a woman, but the demon in his soul, insisting he'd never be enough for anyone to love, relished pushing him toward hell's gate.

"I found out I was pregnant the same day I witnessed the kidnapping. I couldn't risk it, Matt. Trig."

"Risk what? Letting me know I might be the father before you walked away?"

"There was no might about it. You didn't want children. You said."

"Don't care, babe. You should have told me. I could have looked after you, ensured your protection."

"I was in shock. Not thinking straight. You were out of the country, and the FBI suggested WITSEC to keep everyone safe. They swore they'd catch Vokov quickly, and I'd be able to go home."

His blood pressure soared through the roof. Mary was no better than his parents, hiding things they had no business keeping from him.

"I'm sorry." Tears streamed down her face.

"Sorry doesn't cut it, babe," Trig snarled, and stopped pacing. He was making himself fucking dizzy. "What's the kid like?"

Mary fumbled in her pocket for her phone. "Look. She...she has your eyes. And your smile."

An image of the same smiling girl he'd seen earlier looked back at him. Beautiful, like her mom. Too soft and sweet to be a part of him.

Why was she lying? He tore his gaze from the photo. "Save it, babe. What so urgent with your sister?"

Chapter Fifteen

Matt's tone grated as he followed her out of the living room. *Smart move.* Bombarding Matt with six years' worth of stuff he'd missed wasn't helping.

Mary lowered her phone, the one that should have stayed in her pocket. Too much, too soon. The look of awe in his eyes when he saw his daughter swiftly disappeared behind that brick wall between them.

She didn't blame him. Learning you were a father to a child you never knew existed didn't happen every day. The possibility must be a double kick to the balls, considering he never wanted kids.

"Sara, Mary. What the hell is going on?"

"Okay. Bring it down a touch. My head is splitting. She said there was a man watching Lucy in the park. And before you hit blister heat, she's fine, but she needs me, and I've already wasted too long playing doctor with the Walmart first aid kit."

"Your daughter has a stalker. You should have led with that, babe. Grab your coat. My truck's outside."

Alpha vibes the size of a tsunami crashed into her, but she stood her ground and rolled her eyes. "You don't have to come with me? Drop me at the station and I'll catch the next train."

"Thought you were in a hurry."

"Fine." Too tired to argue and feeling light-headed, she would have fallen if he hadn't caught her elbow and steadied her. With a grunt, he guided her to the door. His help. This is what she'd wanted, right? Why she came here to find him? Then why does it feel wrong? Because his concern had nothing to do with fear for *his* daughter. He would protect any child under threat.

Standing at the top of the stairs, the nights of keeping secrets, telling herself she had done the right thing, weighed on her chest, suffocating her. Struggling to breathe, she stared out onto the rainy streets shimmering under the glow of the streetlights.

"Lean on me."

Trig circled his arm around her waist, and she flinched at his sudden change in mood.

"You fall, we detour to E.R. Weight it up, babe. Massive waste of time. Take my arm," he grumbled.

No change then. Grateful for his support, she threaded her hand through the crook at his elbow, as they practically jogged to his truck.

Once they were on the road, Mary closed her eyes, willing the damn to sprout wings. The images of Lucy playing in the park, unaware that anyone wanted to hurt her, looped in her head, killed any chance of falling asleep.

Matt gripped the steering wheel, his focus riveted on the road. The way his dark hair fell across his forehead, the sharp angle of his clenched jaw made him look every inch the brooding movie star.

***

The suggestion he may have a kid hit him hard. A body blow unlike any he'd experienced in the line of duty. Trig hated surprises, for a damn good reason. Like discovering his parents had adopted him right before he enlisted. Massive. Hearing from Knight, his fucking employer, he was most likely a father shattered him. The people close to him, Mary, the folks he called mom and dad, hadn't trusted him with the truth. That hurt. Soul-deep pain.

Mary's light snore, the way her chin rose and fell on her chest with her breath, stirred feelings he couldn't risk feeling again. Not for her.

Not for anyone. She was wrong about the kid's hair. It may be dark like his, but the thick waves shone like her mom's.

Silky strands of her hair hung like a curtain over her shoulders, the way he loved, when she rode him into oblivion. He cleared his throat, hoping she'd stir, open her eyes so he could catch the flecks of gold that glittered in her blue eyes like diamonds in the sun. A beautiful torment.

Despite being forewarned, when she told him about Lucy, he wanted to tear the world apart. If it was true, she'd robbed him of almost six years of watching her grow. Yeah, he said he didn't want kids. Too scared he'd pass on unwanted DNA from his real parents. Whoever the fuck they were. If she'd stuck around, he'd have caved. At least, that's what his gut told him.

She was strong, determined to do things her way. He'd admired the way she fought for those who needed help. Looking at her now, slumped against the window, she looked so damn fragile.

A semi roared past. Mary flinched. A neon motel sign flickered up ahead. Roughly halfway. He signaled and took the exit. Time for his ex to sleep, in a bed, out of the cold. And he needed to get his head straight.

The truck's tires crunched over wet gravel as he pulled into the parking lot. He killed the engine, reached across, and undid her seatbelt. Her smooth skin glistened under the lights, like it used to under the glow of the candles when they made love. A touch of magic, she said, and he'd fallen hard and fast under her spell.

Too much had happened. They weren't the same people, but a little girl was in danger. Right now, they needed him. Whether he liked it or not. He squeezed her slim shoulder. "Hey. Wake up. We're stopping for a few hours."

Her eyes fluttered open, breath catching as she stirred. Confusion clouded the pale blue beauty of her eyes.

"No. We can't stop."

"Yeah. We can. I'm no good to anyone if I fall asleep at the wheel and wrap my truck around a tree. Lucy is safe with Sara," he said firmly. "While you were sleeping, I called the boss, and he sent some-one to watch her house. Inside, you can call her. After we've rested, we'll hit the road again."

Her shoulders slumped. "Okay, two hours. No more."

"Sure." After paying for the night, the receptionist handed over the key to a room at the rear of the building. Unlikely, anyone knew they were there, but he kept his eyes peeled for anything out of place as they walked across the courtyard.

The air was stale inside the room, but the heat worked. It would do for a couple of hours. He flicked on the side lamp. "You take the bed. I'll sleep in the chair."

Mary sank onto the mattress. "That's crazy. Share the bed," she murmured, her small hand patting the space next to her.

"Here's good. Lock the door behind me and take a shower. I'm going to check the place out before I turn in."

When he returned, his gazed locked on the steam floating from the half-open bathroom door. Fuck any chance of shut eye. *Wide awake, here.* Impatient to say hello, his cock nudged the zipper of his jeans. He settled into the chair and waited until Mary appeared.

The motel towel tucked in place under her breasts ended mid-thigh. Wouldn't take much for him to reach her and pile the damn thing at her feet.

He held up his hand to stop her from moving any closer. When that didn't work, he stretched his legs in front of him and folded his arms. "What are you playing at, Mary?"

"Nothing."

Never the truth. Not from her, not from anyone. Where was the dangling something? The unsaid more.

"I'm sorry I hurt you, Matt. I should never have left without speaking to you first."

And that was a fuck ton of more. "Did you love me, Mary?" Because he sure as hell loved her. *Did love, idiot.* Drops of water glistened on her collarbones, and for a moment, he thought of licking them dry.

"I love you, Matt. I never stopped."

His cock twitched at the brush of her hand on his thigh.

"Prove it." Taking hold of her elbows, he lifted her onto his lap. Fucking perfect, the way she straddled his lap. Palms braced against his chest, her core pressed against his arousal. She whimpered. Christ, he loved that sound.

"If we do this, Mary, call it a one time nod to the way it used to be between us. Tell me you understand and that you're okay with that. If not, let's get some sleep."

For a moment, he was sure she meant to head for the bed, but she cupped his cheeks and kissed him. Her lips, as light as a fucking feather, hit him like a sledgehammer.

"I understand."

After six goddam years, were they doing this? *Try stopping me.* Plainly, his cock had no trouble with the idea.

Sliding off his lap onto her knees, her slim fingers undid the button of his jeans, slid down the zipper. He wasn't wearing underwear, but she knew that. Taking him in hand, she started to pump. "You sure about this?" he groaned and clutched the arms of the chair.

"Yes."

His hips bucked at the sparkle in her eyes. Oh, yeah, she wanted him as much as he needed her to get on with it before he came all over her hand. "Lose the towel."

One slow smile and his balls tightened. The towel fell to from her body onto his lap. Taught, dark pink nipples begged for his touch. Who was he to say no? He skimmed the rough pad of his thumb over one nub and then the other before going in for a taste.

"Me first."

Mary bent forward, her hair covering her cheeks. His girl had never shirked from sucking him off. Said she enjoyed it as much as he most certainly fucking did. As she went to her knees, he slid lower into the chair.

A drop of pre-cum slid down the shaft. She swiped it clean with the tip of her tongue and his whole body tensed, a deep groan rolling through his chest.

Eyes fixed on his cock, she reached between her thighs and pinched her clit. *Fuck me.* "Here, let me help." Tall man, long arms. It didn't take much to take over, and for a ball busting minute, eyes closed, she pinched her breasts and enjoyed the ride.

"No. Stop. I said, me first, and I meant it. Stand up."

He prayed his knees didn't buckle, and he did as she asked.

"I've missed this," she sighed.

One hand guided his cock into her sweet, sexy mouth, while the other cupped his balls and squeezed. *Jesus!*

Chapter Sixteen

THE EARLY MORNING AIR was crisp, and the sun had no warmth.
A lot like the man standing behind her. They'd said no more
than a few words to each other this morning. Last night had
been yet another mistake, but she didn't regret it. She'd do almost
anything to see her man reach climax. Lose control at her touch,
her tongue.

When he could look her in the eye again, she guessed they'd
talk. For now, she had enough to worry about.

"Easy, babe. Your sister loves me."

Matt reached over her shoulder and knocked on Sara's door.
She envied his confidence and hated the way he insisted on calling
her babe. It didn't suit either of them.

"Three, two, one."

A smile lifted the corners of her mouth as bang on cue the door
opened, and Sara glared at her. Leaning forward, Mary aimed an
air kiss over her shoulder and grinned at the smudge of bright
blue paint tattooed on her forehead. *Oh, Lucy, my angel. What
have you been up to?*

"Finally," Sara snapped. "I was beginning to think you decided
not to come."

Matt huffed.

Sis turned and stalked into the house before she could offer a half-hearted apology. The smell of coffee and bacon wafting from the kitchen tore a growl from her empty stomach growl.

"Hungry?" Matt asked.

"Starving."

"Always the charmer, your sister."

The warmth of his palm on the curve of her lower back was comforting, despite the way he'd behaved back at the motel.

"I've been up since five, watching the street for any sign of that creep we saw at the park," Sara announced, slamming dishes onto the granite counter. "But sure, take your sweet time getting here. It's not like your daughter's safety is at stake or anything."

"That's on me," Matt stepped forward, his voice carrying the quiet authority that made people pay attention. "I insisted we stop for the night. I was about to fall asleep at the wheel. Hi, I'm Matt McCall. Remember me?"

Fabulous man. Leave it to Matt to put Sara back in her box. Mary had to admit she had no idea why she was ignoring him.

Shaking her wet hands into the sink, her lips curved into the for-men-only smile Mary recognized from their teens. Oh, yeah, sis remembered Matt.

"How could I forget? Do you want coffee?"

"Thanks. Make that two."

And now she wanted to kiss his grumpy ass. With a huff, her sister tucked a loose strand of hair behind her ear. Matt's lips quirked, but his shoulders were tense, and his eyes kept checking the doorway. Expecting the bad guys, or was the grown man scared to meet a six-year-old?

Sara poured them everyone a dark brew. Even as a teenager, she'd loved her strong dose of morning caffeine.

"Anyone want to hear about the creep who scared me half to death?"

Perched on one of two stools at the kitchen island, she peered over the rim of her mug. All about her. Of course it was.

"Cut the crap, Sara. Have you seen him again? I understood Mary asked you not to leave the house until she got here." Matt took her elbow and edged her onto the other stool.

"I heard her, but some of us work. Yesterday, we drove to the office and back. We didn't see him, but I felt him. He was out there. I'm sure of it."

A chill settled in Mary's bones. What if they had seen him? What was her plan? Thank Christ, Matt had someone watching out for them.

"Okay, ladies. Ease up." He slammed his cup on the counter. "Sara, the day in the park, tell me what you remember."

Sara huffed, obviously not mad about repeating herself. Thanks to the tiny feet padding down the hall, she was spared the effort. *Show time.*

Dressed in her favorite unicorn pajamas, Lucy stood in the doorway, rubbing sleepy eyes. Messy dark curls framed her sleepy face. In the morning, she'd give them a brush and braid them with the pretty ribbons she loved.

"Mommy?" Lucy ran to her.

Their daughter wasn't shy, but as soon as she spotted Matt, she hid behind her. At six foot plus, her dad must seem like a giant. Mary's heart softened when he dropped to one knee, immediately taking care of any threat. Grabbing her hand, Lucy took a step closer to him.

A million words bubbled inside her. How do you introduce a father to the daughter he never knew he had? Tears hacked at the back of her throat. Lucy's small world was about to get a hell of a lot bigger.

Thick as honey and just as sticky, the silence stretched between them as father and daughter stared at each other, neither ready to make the first move. Matt's sharp intake of breath did weird things to Mary's insides, made her want to throw her arms around them both and kiss every inch of them.

"Hi, I'm Trig. What's your name, pretty girl?"

"Lucy Lane. This is my mommy."

"We've met, poppet."

***

Trig could not move if the survival of the universe depended on it. His eyes were glued to the fairy, clutching Mary's hand. Cute as, she checked him out, her laser focus taking in every inch of him. Good girl. Wide, curious eyes—his eyes? A part of him wanted to believe Mary, but no one as beautiful as this angel came from his darkness.

"Lucy," Mary said softly, kneeling beside them. "This is your..."

Trig shook his head.

"Er. This is mommy's friend, Trigger."

Sensing the tension, the kid buried her face against her mom's thigh. *Way to go, asshole.*

Lucy tilted her head. "You have a big owie," she said, pointing to the scar on his cheek he'd forgotten was there. The ricochet wound had happened when he joined the military straight out of high school. He chuckled. "Yeah, I do."

"Does it hurt?"

Her tiny fingers brushed his cheek. "Nah. Not anymore."

She nodded, the frown on her face too deep for her age.

"This is Floppy Hop. He had an owie, but Mommy fixed him." He keeps monsters away.

Lucy waved a fluffy toy rabbit in front of his face. His throat tightened as he gently shook the rabbit's paw. "It's nice to meet you, Floppy Hop. Glad you're feeling better."

Without warning, the kid threw her arms around his neck, and his whole body stiffened. Afraid he'd crush her fragile body with the rollercoaster of emotions racing through him, slowly, carefully, he wrapped his arms around her tiny frame.

A fierce war, like nothing he'd encountered in the field, raged inside him. He didn't want to let her go. The need to protect her from every danger the world dared to throw at her raging through every cell in his body.

Forget Vokov. Trig never knew his birth parents. What if they were murderers, drug dealers, or worse? For him to have been taken into care, they must have been real no hopers.

What if his DNA carried their darkness? He'd never risk messing up an innocent child. He pulled back from Lucy's smile. The curve of her lips, the dimples. As jaw dropping gorgeous as her mom's.

Mary stared at them. The mix of hope and fear in her eyes begging him to reassure her everything was okay, all forgiven, but he just couldn't do it.

"Why don't you show Trigger your favorite book, sweetie?" Mary suggested.

"I told her to put them away," Sara muttered.

"I know where they are."

The kid scampered off to fetch her book. His chest swelling with pride at her spunk. *That's my girl. She is not yours.*

"Matt," Mary began, but he cut her off.

"This doesn't change anything," he said, his voice low and strained. "Once we find and deal with Vokov, you and Lucy need to disappear. Start over somewhere I can't find you."

Mary's eyes flashed with hurt and anger. "Why? It's not fair to Lucy or you."

"She, Lucy, deserves better." *Better than me. Now, who's sharing half a story, jerk off?*

Saved by the sound of Lucy returning. He fell to his knees again as she shoved a well-worn picture book into his hands. "Story, please."

"Sure thing, kiddo." With a sigh, Trig scooped Lucy into his arms, swept past Sara and sank onto the couch. One arm wrapped around her waist he snuggled the kid's cheek to his chest and opened the book.

Fear of what he might pass on to this precious bundle if she did turn out to be his daughter, he wasn't convinced, hung in the back of his mind. Yet every time he turned the page, Lucy giggled, a corner of the metal cage containing his heart melted.

Chapter Seventeen

THE DAMN WIND HADN'T stopped howling, rattling the windows and doors of Sara's clapboard home. She lived in a great area, but how the hell did she sleep through the noise in winter?

Playing nice with her grumpy sister and dealing with Matt's indifference all day had been exhausting, but after trying for hours to get comfortable and sleep, Mary gave up and slipped out of bed.

Lucy didn't stir. With Floppy Hop tucked under her chin, she slept peacefully. Not a care in the world, if it wasn't for the telltale thumb in her mouth. Worried for her precious little girl, she kissed her rosy cheek and promised to do better.

I'm starving. At dinner, she didn't eat much. Too scared she wouldn't be able to keep anything down. "I'll be right back," she whispered in Lucy's ear, and avoiding any creaky floorboards, she tiptoed to the kitchen.

Pinching the handle of the cupboard above the bench top, she eased it open. *Christ on a stick.* With the amount of food packed on the shelves, they could survive a nuclear invasion. Unfortunately, snacks didn't rate a mention on the shopping list. Not a cookie or cracker in sight.

In their teens, Sara had turned her nose up at anything sugary. *She's allergic to chocolate.* Mary chuckled. It wasn't one of her finer moments, but she had teased her about it. Mainly, because it had been one of the few ways to crack their parents' perfect angel.

Eventually, she found an open box of Cheerios tucked behind the kitchen towel. How hard did Lucy beg before Sara gave in and bought them?

After adding milk until the bowl almost overflowed, she perched on a stool and took her first bite. Eyes closed, lost in the sugary comfort, she didn't hear Sara enter the kitchen.

"What are you doing?" Sis demanded.

"Nothing." She shrugged and filled the spoon.

"Looks like something to me." Sara stared at the empty box on the island.

"Then why ask, if you know?" Damn it. Trapped. Set up for goddam failure. Like a kid caught with the Easter Egg on Good Friday, she stuffed her face.

"There's no need to lie, Mary. I can shop tomorrow. So long as I know we need more."

What the... "Please, Sara. Not now. I'm tired." *And every bone in my body aches.* "At two a.m., I didn't think a bowl of cereal worth a lengthy discussion. And I'm happy to shop."

Her sister cleared her throat. The way dad used to, right before he passed judgement. The angry-sad moment opened the door to a torrent of ugly memories, and a tear rolled over her cheek. "Why didn't anyone believe me, Sara?"

"What are you talking about?" Her sister turned her back to her and dabbed at a smudge on the refrigerator door, and suddenly Mary was fourteen again, standing in her parents' living room, feeling ignored and alone. "Uncle Jack," she choked on his name. "Just like now, when I told everyone what he did to me, you all said I was lying. Worse, if I was telling the truth, I must have asked for what he did to me." She watched as the color drained from Sara's face.

"Mary, that was years ago. We didn't..."

"Didn't what? Didn't think Jacko was a child molesting monster?" Mary clutched the lip of the island bench, trying not to scream. "No, you blamed me."

"For God's sake Mary. I was young. I didn't understand."

Sara picked up the dishcloth and scooped cereal crumbs into her hand. "You were nineteen." Her damn tears robbed any chance of staying on top of this conversation. Why the hell had she started it in the first place? "Mom and Dad thought the sun shined out of his ass."

"No need to be crude, and you can't blame them. Mom's brother was a wealthy, successful businessman. Gave money to charity."

"So, they assumed I asked him to put his fingers up my skirt and into my underwear?"

"No!" Sara lowered her gaze.

Something, at least. Even a pinch of shame made Mary feel vindicated. Snatching a tissue from the bench top, she blew her nose and placed her half empty cereal bowl in the sink.

"They... they thought you were confused, or wanting attention. Uncle Jack was great with kids, spoiled us, took us on outings. What you were accusing him of didn't fit with the man they knew."

"Seriously, I was the troublemaker?"

Sara shrugged. "You were the one who loved the drama. Not that much of a stretch to think you were making it up."

Go to hell. Mary kept going, her words coming faster now the dam had broken. "Do you remember how it was growing up, Sara? Dad with his company, Mom with her charity work and social obligations. You, the perfect daughter, a straight-A student, captain of the debate team, never a hair out of place. And then there was me."

Sara huffed. "Wild, unpredictable Mary, always in trouble at school, breaking the rules."

"I was desperate for them to see me, not as a problem, but as a child who needed them. I swore then my child would never feel alone." Her voice hitched.

Sara's eyes widened with dawning realization. "Mary, I didn't realize..."

"No, you didn't," she cut in, but the anger had vanished, replaced by deep, aching sadness. "None of you did. To be fair, when Uncle Jack started paying attention to me, showing an interest in my life, my hobbies... God forgive me, Sara, I was so starved for adult approval, for someone to make me feel special."

Like she'd done as a child, many times in WITSEC, Mary wrapped her arms round her waist and gave herself a hug. "That bastard took that need, that vulnerability, and twisted it into something ugly. And when I found the courage to speak up, to ask for help, you all assumed I was attention seeking in the worst possible way."

"Okay. We should have seen you were in trouble."

Her sister's face crumpled with guilt.

"Yes. But you didn't. And when Matt used to tell me how special I was, how much he loved me, there was a part of me that didn't this it was truly possible. That day, faced with staying to tell him what happened, a part of me didn't think he'd believe me, so I chose to protect our unborn child and leave. How fucked is that?"

"Sara."

"No. Don't you dare pull me up on my language?"

"Mommy?"

Lucy's small voice sliced through the anger threatening to destroy any connection between them.

"Mommy, why are you crying?"

Oh, God. Matt stood in the doorway, cradling Lucy in his arms. She forced a smile. "It's okay, sweetie. Mommy and Aunt Sara were just talking. Let's get you back to bed." Matt didn't resist when she scooped Lucy from his hold.

As she passed, the pain and regret in her sister's eyes struck her, but it was too late. Damage done.

Lucy was asleep by the time she finished tucking her into bed. She brushed the hair from her face and snuggled Floppy Hop back under her chin. Facing Matt and Sara was way too hard, so she slipped off her shoes and lay on the bed beside her, content to count her daughter's breaths. She loved Lucy more than her life. "I'll never let anyone hurt you, sweetie."

Chapter Eighteen

Both hands wrapped around the mug Sara had slammed in front of her a few seconds ago, Mary inhaled the smell of strong coffee and wished she was light years from Boston.

Opposite, Lucy looked right at home, sitting on Matt's knee, tapping the top of her boiled egg. Earlier he'd nudged a fresh box of Cheerios in her direction. He had driven to the store to buy them before anyone else was awake.

Taking another sip of her coffee, she tried not to be obvious about checking out his handsome face. Sure, he was older, the creases on his forehead and the spidery lines framing his mouth hadn't been there before. She had a few herself. And that mouth. From what she remembered, his exceptionally talented mouth. They hadn't spoken about the other night, and she doubted they ever would.

"Want some soldiers to dip in your egg, Lucy?" she asked. The way her kids' eyes lit up made her smile.

"Can I have grown up toast? Please," she added, pointing at the rack in front of her.

"Sure, sweetie. Want me to butter it for you?"

"No, thank you. Trigger, will you do it?"

"No problem poppet." Matt said, hesitating before she gave him an okay nod.

"Be my guest."

With a wink, he buttered the slice on both sides and cut it in half. His huge hand dwarfed Lucy's as he handed her the buttery treat.

"Thank you." She giggled.

Wow. Did he blush? Had to be a trick of the light or her kid was having more success at touching his heart.

"Pleasure's all mine, poppet. More?"

Lucy wiggled her backside and peered at her. "Mommy says not too much bread, more egg."

Matt cleared his throat. "Right."

The two of them were adorable. "Okay. One more slice." She pushed the toast rack toward him.

Sara hadn't moved from the kitchen window where she'd been for the past ten minutes. Feeling sheepish about losing it last night, Mary collected the plates and brought them over to the sink. "Everything okay, Sara. Why don't you sit down, and I'll make a fresh pot of coffee."

"No, thanks." She shook her head and turned off the taps. "I just saw the man from the park coming from around the back of the house."

Her sister stood on tiptoe to get a better look. Heart pounding, hand resting on Sara's shoulder, she did the same. A guy walked swiftly alongside the fence, heading for the end of the drive. He wore a dark hoodie and kept his head down, making it impossible to see his face.

"Get away from the damn window." Matt shouted and lifted Lucy off his knee.

"Mommy," Lucy wailed.

"Hey," she growled at Matt. Great that he cared, but he'd scared her. "It's okay, sweetie." Lucy ran into her open arms.

"Sorry," Matt mumbled.

"Hey! Who are you? What do you want?" Sara flung open the back door and stormed out after the guy.

Mary followed. *Damn.* Without breaking stride, he headed straight for them. Not hanging around for his answer, she grabbed Sara's arm and dragged her back to the house.

"Get inside! Take care of Lucy," Matt shouted, sprinting past them.

The guy bolted and leaped into a waiting car. Black with tinted windows. The engine roared to life.

"Stay in the house. Lock the doors and call 911."

Matt yelled over his shoulder at her, raced to his truck, and took off after the sedan.

***

Motherfucker. Trigger floored the accelerator. Up ahead, the sedan weaved through downtown traffic. A few more seconds and he'd be close enough to read the number plate. Keeping one hand on the wheel, he drew out his phone and attached it to the car speaker.

"Sentinel Security. This is Linda. How can I help you?"

"Hey. It's Trig. Put me through to Snake."

"And good morning to you, too. You guys need to—"

"Now. Linda." Their receptionist irritated the hell out of him. Why Snake kept her on, he didn't know. At least he wouldn't have to put up with her for much longer.

"What's up, man? Winter said you were on your way to Boston. Family, okay?" Snake asked.

Not my family. "Fuck no. Sara, Mary's sister, reported some guy watching the kid in the park. This morning, the son of a bitch showed up at her house. I'm in pursuit. Dark sedan, tinted windows, heading north out of Boston."

"Copy that. What's your position?"

"Heading East on Alwin Street, heading toward the I-90. Look, I know you're too far away to assist, but have Hawke run this plate ASAP." He rattled off the number.

"On it. Hang on."

"Shit." Trigger's world tilted sideways as a school bus pulled out from the side street to his left. Trying to avoid a collision, he wrenched the wheel to the right and hit the brakes. For a heart-stopping moment, he panicked, sure he would clip the bus's rear.

By some miracle, his truck skidded to a halt inches from disaster. The sedan's taillights swam into the sea of traffic. "Dammit!" Trigger slammed his palm against the dash.

"Trig, you still there?" The boss sounded concerned.

"Yeah, I'm here." He cursed. "Lost visual on the target. Near miss with a bus. Any luck on that plate?"

"Negative. The plate comes up blank."

Trigger's stomach churned. "Damn it."

"Most likely stolen. Hawke's on it."

"Thanks. I'm heading back to the house. Let me know when you hear."

"Roger that. Stay frosty."

Snake chuckled. "Yeah. Will do." Thoughts racing, he turned the car around. A deep sense of unease rolling through every cell in his body.

There were two cop cruisers parked outside Sara's by the time he made drove up the driveway and parked. He'd almost made it to the front steps when Mary crashed through the screen door. Her face was ashen, her limp pronounced. "What part of stay inside didn't you understand?" He grabbed her elbow and pulled her inside.

Seated at the kitchen table, Sara was talking to an officer. Oblivious, Lucy sat on the floor with her coloring books. Mary shrugged off his hand and scooped her into her arms. Their eyes met.

"Did you catch him?" she asked.

He shook his head. "Lost him."

Her shoulders slumped. *Yeah, you and me both, honey.*

Half an hour later, after giving his statement, the cops agreed to swing by during their night rounds, and Trig showed them out. After he checked in with his team and made sure Snake had someone looking out for Sara, he planned on taking Mary and Lucy far away from Boston. His cabin in upstate New York was isolated, defendable. Much easier to protect them there.

"You and Lucy can't stay here," he said quietly. "It's not safe."

Mary nodded. Still shaken, her eyes darted to where her sister sat. "Sara has to come, too."

"Safer if she's not with you." He was good at what he did. America had spent a fuck ton honing his deadly skills, but the fewer people he had to protect, the better for them. Until they found out how Vokov knew their every move, he'd keep on coming. Of that, he was certain.

"Where will you go?" Sara asked.

"Best you don't know that way, you can't tell." When her breath hitched, he added, "Don't worry. You'll be safe, here. Sentinel will keep watch."

"No. I'm not leaving you."

Mary narrowed her eyes at him. Still holding Lucy, she sat on the couch.

And why the fuck not? After what he'd overheard last night. But that was his Mary. *Not mine. Not anymore.* A warrior champion when it came to taking care of the underdog. Time for someone to take care of her for a change. Something she should have trusted him to do six damn years ago.

"Not gonna argue, babe. Up you get. I'll help you pack, poppet." Low blow, reaching for the kid. Lucy hopped off her mom's knee and grabbed his hand. He had no doubt if Mary had a weapon right now, he'd be a dead man.

Chapter Nineteen

"Let go of my hand, Matt. I don't need your help packing our things." Ordinarily, Mary craved his touch. When they first met, he loved to take the lead. Unlike now, she never resented his grumpy alpha ass. If leaving meant protecting Lucy, she'd go wherever he wanted. "You don't have to herd me like a prize heifer."

"Sorry." Matt released her.

"Come on, pumpkin, help mommy pack." She bent to pick Lucy up and was surprised when she pulled away, too.

"It's okay, mommy. I can walk."

Her gaze darted from her to her dad, who couldn't stop the corners of his mouth from riding an upswing.

"I don't want to go. I want to play." Lucy pouted and batted her baby blues at Matt.

Stubborn. And who did that remind her of? "I know, baby, but we're going on vacation," she blurted the first thing that came into her head.

"Disney World?" Lucy's cheeks glowed at the possibility.

"Maybe, baby." She glared at Matt. *A little help here.*

"Okay, with me, poppet. I know a great store that sells the best fairy princess dresses. Perfect for a Magic Kingdom." He grinned.

Lucy allowed his huge hand to swallow her tiny fingers and lead her to the bedroom.

"Underwear. Socks. Shirt. Pants. Shoes." Matt ordered.

Mary chuckled and waited for Lucy to sit her little backside on the floor and refuse to move. Her heart swelled when her kid giggled and stretched her arms out for a boost to reach the top drawer.

She finished gathering their toiletries from the bathroom while they left to gather up her toys. After a last look to check they hadn't forgotten anything, she was turning to join them when the doorbell rang.

"Mary? Go to mom, poppet" Matt guided Lucy toward her.

One hand reaching for the gun she'd seen tucked into the back of his jeans, she trembled as he moved to the door.

"Trig You in there?"

"It's okay." Matt pulled his tee over the holster and opened the door. "Thanks for coming man."

Like all the Sentinel men, he was big like Matt, though not as tall. Strong and muscular, the military oozing out of him. Good looking, but nowhere as drop-dead gorgeous as Matt. He winked at Lucy, who did her usual trick of playing peek-a-boo from behind her leg.

"Afternoon, ma'am." Dex looked directly at her sister and lowered his chin.

"Sara. Come in, come in," she said, her face lighting up.

Taking his hand, her sister dragged Dex over the threshold. Mary smiled. Before she went into WITSEC, her sister hadn't shown much interest in men, but one look at super hunk and she was blushing like a teenager.

✳✳✳

Amazing. Taking in Mary's grin at the connection between Sara and Dex, Trigger fell more in love, if that was even a thing, with the woman who played tug-o-war with his heart.

Even after what he'd heard last night, she insisted Sara came with them. Putting her sister first. Almost as if she believed she didn't deserve to be a priority. He'd fix that. After they had a long talk. Sooner rather than later.

"Time to move." The plan was to swap his truck with Dex's SUV. More comfortable and faster. Gain time before Vokov figured out the switch. "All set?" *Far from it.* Mary needed more rest. Once they reached the cabin, he'd make sure she crashed for at least twenty-four hours.

"Yes."

Before she could grab their bags, he scooped Lucy off the floor with one arm and grabbed them. "I've got this."

Dex followed them out, head on a swivel as Matt loaded the bags into the trunk and secured Lucy's car seat. "Up you go, poppet." He secured her seatbelt.

Mary had said her goodbyes, but she hesitated. Getting ready to change her mind, he could see it in her eyes. Reaching for the door handle, he opened it and helped her into the passenger seat. "Sara will be fine. Dex won't let anything happen to her. Right now. We need to focus on keeping you and Lucy safe. You matter."

Mary met his gaze, surprise flickering in her eyes. Doubt he'd put there. *Yeah. That talk was long overdue.* "Fasten your seatbelt?"

"Done. Now get in and drive before I bawl eyes out and make a complete idiot of myself."

Lucy was snoring before they made it to the interstate. Her small face, peaceful, unaware of the danger, and he planned to keep it that way.

"Everyone warm enough?" Trig asked to break the silence. No conversation, only the silent rhythm of Mary glancing in the rearview mirror, checking on Lucy, while he scanned the same goddam mirror for any sign they were being followed.

To hell with the cabin. He wanted to load them into a spaceship, head for the moon, and start over. Just the three of them. Lucy's Magic Kingdom was rubbing off on him.

Ever since Mary walked back into his life, the darkness, the loneliness he'd felt after she disappeared, began fading. And there wasn't a goddam thing he could do about it. Their chance at happiness had come and gone, but he'd keep them safe or die trying.

"Where exactly are we going?" Mary asked, her voice thin, tired.

He couldn't stop himself, didn't even try. He reached across the center console, curled his fingers around her slim thigh, and gave it a reassuring squeeze. "My cabin. Outside of Rochester."

He bought it the year after Mary left him. To recoup after missions, he told himself. To brood more like it. Sit for hours on the damn porch with a bottle of bourbon. At home with his fucking demons, indulging the rage that never went away. "It's isolated. I can protect you there until this is done.

Mary nodded. "Can we pull over? I want to get in the back with Lucy."

"Sure. But why not let her sleep?"

"Matt? What are we doing?" She nodded at his hand on her thigh and sighed.

Fucked if he knew. Things were moving way too fast. For him. For her? "What happened to your knee?"

Her whole body tensed. The question had been burning a hole in his skull, and, okay, this wasn't how he'd intended finding out. Jealous that a five-year-old deserved Mary's attention more than he did, the thought of her shifting to the back gutted him.

"That day, there was a struggle. The man who tried to kidnap Tilly was hurting her. I couldn't let that happen, so I tried to stop him. Stupid. I know. He went to grab me, and I fell. Before I could get to my feet, he stomped on my leg, fracturing my kneecap and causing extensive ligament damage. It bothers me when I don't get enough sleep or I'm not doing my exercises.

The flat tone in her voice, as if she was giving him over her fucking grocery list, tore at his insides. "He will pay."

"Oh, he did. The police shot him. Dead at the scene. It was Vokov's brother, Maxim."

Chapter Twenty

HANDS CLASPED BEHIND HIS back, Vokov gravitated to his favorite place in the room. If he were staying longer, he'd have a gold X made to mark the spot where he could stand like a king looking out of the floor-to-ceiling windows at Manhattan.

A long way from Ingushetia, where he grew up. His family *bratva* royalty. As a child, they moved around, stayed ahead of the few *politsiya* with a hero's death wish who refused to accept their bribes.

For many reasons, not all business, he didn't want to leave America. He had no choice, thanks to the bitch social worker who killed Maxim. But not before she paid.

He sculled the last of his Beluga Gold and placed the glass on the coffee table. He missed an open fireplace where he could smash his glass and celebrate Mary Lane and her daughter's death.

His lover slouched against the bar. The constant drumming of his fingers on the polished marble was annoying. However, the sound had its advantages, as it made him look at the man. A sight that more than made up for the irritation.

A strand of his shiny black hair fell across his forehead. Longer than usual, like many of his countrymen, he favored the short back and sides. Vokov preferred this way, something to grip when they fucked.

Any other time, the cocky grin on his perfect lips meant the start of hot, sweaty sex. Tonight, neither he nor his cock were sure if they still liked the man. "Your employee is late." Reaching for the silver lighter his *dedushka* had given him on his thirteenth birthday, he lit another cigarette. Grandfather believed in starting everything early.

"Parking?" his lover drawled.

Vokov chuckled. "No doubt you're right, my friend." This was Manhattan.

As if waiting for their cue, the elevator doors opened and a scrawny figure, assisted by two of his bodyguards, stumbled into the apartment.

One of his arms dangled monkey-style at his side while the fingers of the other fumbled with his shirt collar. Sweat poured from his brow. He looked as though he hadn't slept in days and shifted, rat-like, from one foot to the other. It made him nauseous, but he'd be damned if he'd ask the rodent to sit.

"Ah, good of you to join us. Mr. Tumbler." He latched his gaze onto the liability and dragged long and slow on his cigarette.

"Tumbler will do."

The idiot cocked his head to the side, as if raising his chin somehow warranted respect. He was tempted to ask if he got the name because he often got kicked down the stairs.

"Very well, Tumbler. I hear you've had an eventful week."

"Mr. Vokov, boss, I can explain—" His Adam's apple bobbed.

"No need." Waving his hand at one of the leather armchairs, he nodded at the bodyguards. "Sit." Leaning against the bar next to his lover, he brushed his lover's arm with the tip of his index finger. "I must say, *Rodnaya,* I'm rather disappointed with Tumbler's progress."

"Mr. Vokov. Please. I can explain," Ratty whined.

"Shh. Where are my manners? Please, Leonid, pour my friend a drink." The bodyguard closest to him did as he was bid. No question, no fuss. As he liked it.

"Thanks. The good stuff." Tumbler grinned and raised his glass of vodka.

"Glad it meets with your approval. Now, tell me what happened. How did you allow a woman and child to slip through your fingers?" His Russian accent thickened.

"Yeah, about that, Boss. Things got complicated. The broad's smart, and she's got some big guy looking out for her."

"Smart? Interesting. Perhaps she could share some of her smarts with you." Grabbing his lover's tie, he plundered his mouth. Long and hard, taking his time to enjoy the combination of alcohol and tobacco on his breath. "You had one job, Tumbler. One," he said, releasing the man standing next to him.

"Like I said, she has help. Nobody said anything about him."

His lover grunted, enjoying the pantomime.

"He's a professional bodyguard from some security company. We should have had her, but..." Tumbler cleared his throat.

"But?" Vokov raised an eyebrow, his patience wearing thin.

"She disappeared. But my men are searching. We'll find her, and next time we'll finish it." His face paled.

"I appreciate initiative in my employees, Tumbler. However, there is only one thing I value more. Can you guess what that is?" He walked over to the bookshelf by the spiral staircase leading to the mezzanine floor and ran his fingers through the gap between two leather-bound books. Another gift from his *dedushka*.

"Er. No. What's that, Boss?" His shoulders hitched with a nervous laugh.

"Competence, Tumbler. Now drink up." He aimed the black handgun he'd retrieved from between the books at the ratty rodent.

Tumbler's fingers lost their grip on his glass, and he tried to stand. The bodyguards moved swiftly to prevent him. "Boss, wait."

"Contract terminated, *Mister* Tumbler." Vokov aimed the gun at the center of the idiot's forehead and pulled the trigger. "We no longer require your services." The shot reverberated through the room. Tumbler's body jerked, his eyes wide in disbelief, as he slumped against the back of his chair. Blood pooled around him.

Vokov strolled to his desk, retrieved a silk handkerchief from the top drawer and wiped the gun clean before returning it to the bookshelf. He turned to his lover. "Volga's for dinner, *myshka?*" Not the most expensive restaurant in town, but they served his favorite dish. Three caviars with a stack of blinis. Heaven.

"Sure. Now that you've made your point, he drawled, signaling for the bodyguards to take care the mess."

At the glimmer of admiration in the man's eyes, his cock finally stirred. Guess there was still a spark in the relationship. "Change of plan. We will order in."

"Suits me."

"Good. Then tomorrow, you, *myshka,* will find this bitch and her child and bring them to me."

Chapter Twenty-One

It had been a long trip, six, seven hours, with only a brief break for gas and coffee. The sun had set ages ago, and despite Matt cranking up the heat in the car, a bitter chill skipped across Mary's shoulders.

Mary reached between the front seats and tucked the blanket over Lucy's shoulders. She'd been asleep for most of the trip, but restless, kicking her cover off her legs at regular intervals.

"We're almost there. Play is up ahead. How's she doing?" Matt focused on the dark road.

"Good. She's tough, had to be, but being her mom and all, I worry about her. She used to have the occasional nightmare, but lately they're happening almost every night."

Matt inhaled as though he were about to speak. What had he been going to say and didn't? She shrugged and peered out of the side window, trying to catch a glimpse of the cabin.

Several minutes later, a clearing opened up, revealing a sturdy log home surrounded by tall trees. Add a dusting of snow, and they had the perfect setting for a Christmas romcom movie.

The moon popped through the clouds long enough to shine on two weather-beaten Adirondacks sat side by side around a fire pit. Who had Matt shared a cozy evening with over the years?

"Home sweet home." Matt swung the vehicle in a semi-circle and cut the engine.

They couldn't hide forever, zipping up and down the highway, and right now she wasn't looking forward to being a prisoner again. No matter how beautiful the scenery was. A chill gnawed at the base of her spine, along with the certainty Vokov would find them.

Releasing her safety belt, she turned to do the same for Lucy. Her breath caught at the sight of her chubby cheeks flushed with sleep.

"It's going to be okay, Mary. Wait here. I'll open up and do a quick check round back."

Matt squeezed her hand. He'd always been able to read her thoughts. Wishing she shared his confidence, she half-smiled, but she was too scared to fall into the softness she imagined in his voice. The drive had been long.

With the sleeve of her coat, she brushed the condensation from the window and watched him stride toward the cabin. The sight of his muscular thighs bulging against his denim jeans made her mouth water. *You have a mighty fine ass.* She chuckled to herself and closed her eyes and inhaled the crisp, clean air. It sounded like water nearby, but she couldn't be sure.

"All clear. Let's get you two inside."

Matt's voice rumbled in her ear. She opened her eyes and prayed she stayed awake long enough to make it through the door.

"Go on in. It's open. I'll fetch Lucy and come back for the bags."

"It's okay. I'll carry her while you bring our stuff." She expected an eye roll, not the look of disappointment, blended with something else she couldn't put her finger on that made her change her mind. "Thanks. I'm exhausted." When he smiled, it felt deep-down good to give it right back to him.

As though he'd being doing it for years, without waking her, he scooped Lucy out of her seat and tugged the edges of his jacket around her.

"Mommy," she groaned, but her eyes stayed shut.

"I'm here, baby. Sleep." Together, they made their way up the porch steps. Out of place in the idyllic setting, a security pad glowed eerie green on the cabin wall.

"I'll give you the code tomorrow," he said as he punched in a series of numbers, then toed open the squeaky door.

Mary grinned.

"What's funny?" he asked.

"Nothing. Tickled me that your state-of-the-art security door needs oiling."

His deep laugh rumbled in his chest. and Lucy sneezed. "Guess so. Didn't get around to fixing it when I was here last."

She looked for a light switch as he laid Lucy on the leather couch.

"Take this." Matt tossed her a headlamp from the coffee table. "The cabin's off grid."

Spending time with him in candlelight certainly appealed, but with a five-year-old running around the small space tomorrow, not so much. Matt nodded at the shelf in the kitchen.

"There are solar powered led lights, and the refrigerator is gas-powered. I cook outside."

Of course he did. The cabin wasn't big. No need, she guessed. He'd never enjoyed spending too much time indoors. He took her hunting once. Disaster. She refused to watch him kill a living animal.

Her gaze wandered over the rustic, yet comfortable furnishings. The couch faced a stone fireplace, and now her eyes had adjusted, she appreciated the number of windows.

"The guest room is the first door on the left. You'll find extra blankets in the closet. Make yourself at home."

Mary's heart clenched. Home. A short word, packed with a ton of wishes and wants she'd said goodbye to six years ago. She lifted Lucy and almost stumbled when her toe caught the edge of the rug.

"Here. Let me take her."

"Not this time. I need a hug." She smiled at his audible gasp. "From my daughter. How about a fire?"

"Yeah. No problem."

The door opposite the spare room was ajar, open enough to see a king-sized bed covered in deep burgundy sheets and a sheepskin cover. She recognized it as the one that used to cover their bed. Memories of her fingers gripping the soft, creamy wool as they made love sent her libido into hyper drive. Being here in Matt's retreat felt right and wrong at the same time.

The room was freezing. So, she slipped off Lucy's boots, left her socks on, and pulled the covers up to her chin. "Dream of fairies tonight, sweetie. No witches," she whispered and kissed her fore-head.

"Mary?"

Matt stood in the doorway. His tall, solid body filled the frame.

"Wash up. Bathrooms through there." He turned and pointed to the room with the enormous bed. "Fire's going."

"Great. Give me ten. Any chance of a coffee?"

"Sure. And I'll fetch the bags." He drummed his fingers on the door frame, again looking like he wanted to say something more, then left.

Splashing cold water on her face ought to keep her awake long enough to drink a mug before she joined Lucy in her comfortable bed. Honestly, she'd be content sleeping on the floor if it meant stretching her leg.

Wow. The bathroom took her breath away. The shower was enor-mous, but best check the water situation before she promised herself a long soak in the morning. Turning on the tap, she ran a face cloth under the cold water, pressed it to her eyelids, then ran it over her face.

Back in the main living area. Matt was lifting a small painting off the wall next to the fridge and running his fingers over keys on a small panel.

"All set. Motion sensors, cameras. We'll know if anyone broaches the perimeter."

Stifling a yawn, she tilted her head to one side. "Really? I thought you said we were off grid?"

"We are. But Hawke works in mysterious ways."

"Hawke?"

"Sentinel's tech expert. The woman's a witch."

"She sounds indispensable." Mary winced at the hint of the green-eyed monster and stared at the raging fire. "Thank you for bringing us here."

"No stretch. It's what I do."

"Right. Sure." *No reason to think she was special.* Except for those moments when he looked at her, and his whiskey-colored eyes warmed every inch of her. Dumb moments when she hoped they had a chance at being together.

"Come here."

She ought to step away, not melt at his order, but she didn't hesitate. Stepped right into his outstretched arms. Wrapping her arms around his waist, she snuggled into his chest and imagined a different life from the hell she was living. A life with Lucy and the man she had never stopped loving.

A family who ate breakfast together. Enjoyed perfect evenings, curled up by the fire, after they put their girl to bed. Laughter echoing off the log walls. Trips to the Magical Kingdom. A bubble that burst the day Vokov crossed her path.

Chapter Twenty-Two

IT TOOK EVERY OUNCE of control he had left to let her go. What the hell was he thinking taking her in his arms in the first place, but she looked too damn fragile? It didn't take a genius to know she was hurting, and he'd give his world to take away her pain.

"Coffee's ready. You should eat. Tomorrow, I'll cook outside. For tonight, take your pick from the MREs over there."

Mary cocked her head to the side and smoothed her hands over her jeans. "Great. MREs?"

"Meal, Ready-to-Eat. On assignments, we live on them. Can't promise they taste that great, but you won't starve. Chilli Mac is my choice. In the morning, we'll drive to the store for supplies. There's one about ten miles down the road."

"Honestly. I'm not that hungry."

"You look all in." *And I'd love to carry you to bed, have you fall asleep in my arms.* The likelihood anyone knew they were here amounted to zero, but luck had a way of throwing dirt in a man's face. "Eat. I need to bring my team up to speed, then do a perimeter check. He took his phone off the counter and grabbed a jacket from the hook on the door.

"Okay, I'll wait 'til you get back."

"No. Go ahead, might take me a while." Enough time for the wind to shrink his balls and wrangle his dick. "Lock the door. Stay warm."

"Be safe."

He had one foot on the top step, on the point of forgetting the call, when Lucy called out to her. Saved by the poppet who had him twisted around her finger. "Always, now go on, inside."

He scrubbed a hand through his hair and punched in Snake's number. His breath curled in the night air as he waited for him to answer. Normal shit. A SITREP. *Yeah. When has anything concerning Mary been normal?* Through the window, he saw her pacing. "Eat", he mouthed when she caught his eye.

"Wondered when you'd get around to calling," Snake grumbled. "Everything okay with you and your girl?"

"She's not my girl."

"Yeah right. My bad. Everyone okay?"

"All things considered. Lucy's handling it better than the grownups." His lips quirked. "Anything more from Hawke?" His skin crawled at the pause on the other end of the line.

"She's chasing a couple of leads. Caught Vokov on camera, boarding a flight to Chicago. Used a fake passport, as you fucking do. There's chatter he's heading for a meetup with major buyers."

"How's Sara?" Mary was bound to ask, and he didn't want to disappoint.

"I've sent Storm to join him. In case you need us, Winter and I will continue to stand by in the city."

"Thanks, Boss." Good to know his team had his back. Hawke was moving in the right direction, but he'd rest easier when she had something more definite for them to go on. "Keep me posted."

"Will do. Don't take so long before you call next time. You'll have me worried."

"Yeah, yeah. I'll check in again in the morning." Trig shoved his phone into his pocket and finished his checks. No sign of any intruders on the property. Too goddam quiet. If it wasn't here yet, trouble was on its fucking way. His gut never lied.

Recon completed, he took the shortcut through the trees and headed for the cabin. As soon as he set foot inside, he spotted the uneaten MREs on the counter. "You didn't eat."

"Very observant."

Sitting on the floor in front of the fire, Mary looked at him, her cute grin mocking the hell out of him. "Fine. Get some rest. Take my bed. I'll sleep in here. Keep watch in case we have any unexpected visitors."

"If you're sure?"

He nodded. "Goodnight, Mary."

"Nite Trig."

As she passed, their arms brushed, and a jolt of electricity zapped over his skin. She'd felt it, too. He'd insisted she not call him by his first name, but his call sign sounded wrong on her lips.

Close to breaking point, he was a fucking breath from telling her he'd never be anyone else, but her Matt, and no way did she get to walk away from him again.

Foot twitching, determined not to march after her and drag her across the gigantic chasm between them, he watched her leave. The coffee was cold, but he drank it and settled into the armchair facing the door. Jus picturing Mary lying naked in his bed, his cock throbbed. Outside, the trees whispered, inside the cabin creaked and sighed with the weight of the unspoken stuff between them.

Any other time he'd have taken himself in hand, but with a kid in the house, who knew when poppet might go for a wander. After making sure his weapon was within reach, he settled in for a one-eye-half-open night with a serious case of blue balls.

It wouldn't take much to change his mind and snuggle up behind Mary, slide his fingers between her legs and set the whole fucking world on fire. *No invitation, buddy*. And he didn't expect one anytime soon.

After an hour of tossing and turning, he gave in and made another pot of coffee. He was on his second mug when Mary limped into view.

"You, okay? Your leg. Are you in pain? There's Tylenol in my bag if you need it."

"No, thanks. And I'm not the only one who needs rest." Her gaze landed on his coffee.

"It's hot. Want one? Found the creamer if you take it."

"Sure."

Mary stepped closer to the fire. Beating her there, lifted the pot off the hob. "Sit." He tossed his chin at the couch.

"Matt, I... I'm so sorry," she blurted.

He raised an eyebrow at the slip. Not really feeling it, but it happened.

"Sorry. Trigger sounds weird. I'll try harder. It doesn't change anything, but I want you to know how much I..." she faltered.

"What?" *Selfish prick. Yeah, but I want to hear it.*

"How much I, Lucy, needs you."

Heart thumping in his chest, Matt blinked a couple of times. Why? Because big boys cry too, and he wasn't about to let it happen.

"I wish... I wish things were different." She raced to the finish. "I need you..."

As if the flames had the power to incinerate six years of missing her, he stoked the fire. From drowning his sorrows, to volunteering for the most dangerous missions on offer, he'd done everything he knew how to forget Mary Maud. Stop her living in his head every minute of the goddam day. Nothing worked.

Whatever demon lived inside him burned for her touch, demanded he have her. One time, be damned. Two strides and he towered over her, lifting her off the couch and into his arms. Her sex pressed against his arousal. Her strong thighs gripped his torso with the strength of a steel vise. "Hold on," he growled against her ear.

He ought to check if she was sure. After she did the honors last time, they'd agreed never again, but he was too damn scared she'd insist this was a mistake. Her eyes glistened. The soft circle of her arms around his neck tightened. *Maybe, just maybe.*

"I want this. You?"

Hell the fuck yeah. Lifting her higher, he pressed her back into the wall and rocked his hips against hers, praying she had her answer.

The second her lips parted, he nipped her bottom lip, slid inside her mouth and sucked her tongue. "Mmm. You taste good," he murmured. *Sweet.* Taking a breath, he dived back in for a second taste.

Her hand over his heart, her whimper as he slipped his hand under her sweater and traced the silky, soft skin between each rib, undid and bound him to her at the same time. The scent of her arousal begged him to come closer. He laid a trail of kisses across her throat, between her breasts, and sucked a nipple between his teeth.

Years ago, Mary had stepped inside his skin and never left. Locked in his DNA, she had a home in every cell of his body. Always had. But losing her had almost finished him.

Trig pulled back, creating enough space to look her in the eye. Her gaze penetrated every corner of his darkness.

"Please. I need this." She ran the tip of her finger along the seam between his lips.

"I'm not sure," he mumbled, wishing to Christ he could do better.

"I am. Be strong for me, Matt. I miss you."

Wide eyed, her thighs gripped him harder as she rubbed against his cock. Hell, if she kept it up, he'd come in his goddam pants. "Miss you too, sweetheart." Leaning forward, he kissed her eyelids and prayed he had the strength to love her the way she deserved.

Aware Lucy might poke her head out at any moment, he carried her to his bedroom and kicked the door closed. Once inside, he lay her gently on the bed.

Eyes open wide, her gaze reached inside and looked deep into everything was. He loved the way she allowed him to take the lead. One knee on the bed, he pulled his top over his head and reached for the hem of her sweater.

"Let me." She grinned, pulling it off and tossing it over his head.

Desperate to see her naked, he pulled her jeans and panties off in one move. Reaching underneath her slim frame, he unclasped her bra. No trendy Victoria's Secret for Mary. Plain silk bras in flesh pink with matching panties that made him drool. Some things never changed. "Wow," he groaned his approval as he itched to stroke and bite her smooth, pale skin.

An answering moan, edged with frustration, rolled from her lips as she tugged on his belt buckle. "Allow me." Pushing back onto his feet, he shucked his pants and jocks.

"Wow," she teased.

A strand of hair fell across her face, and she blew it away. Hell, he'd add the move to a permanent loop just to see that glazed look of approval every day of the week. She bounced when he leaped onto the bed and muffled her giggle with her hands.

"Lucy," she reminded him.

His tongue lathed her nipple, then switched to her other breast and grazed it with his teeth. When her hands roamed over his chest, her fingers tugging on the hairs on his chest, his cock swelled against her belly.

"Please, Matt. I don't want to wait," she groaned.

On that, they were on the same page. He'd never stopped needing Mary. Her calm, her warmth. He used to dream of seeing her after a mission. Being in her arms was the only time he felt real peace. His palms curved over her hips. Easing back slightly, his tongue swirled inside the well of her navel.

"Oh, God."

Trig thrust his knee between her thighs and parted her legs. *Sweet Jesus.* For the love of all things holy, he wanted more than his next breath when her fingers curled around his shaft, and she placed the tip of his cock at her entrance. Their gazes locked. Holding her still, he rocked his hips and sank to the hilt inside her wet heat.

"So tight, baby." He wanted to move, but he didn't want to hurt her. Big guy, not going to have a tiny dick, and Mary was petite, delicate. His heart pounded. He needed slow. Time to enjoy making love to the woman who owned him, body and soul.

Eyes closed, he held onto what little control he had left, telling himself to go slow, enjoy making love to the woman who owned him, body and soul. Until she dug her fingers into his scalp and held onto her scream. The feel of her warm breath on the side of his neck was magic. Small, sharp teeth nipped his earlobe.

Mine. The word, the truth, roared in his ears. "I've got you, sweetheart. Hold on."

He pulled out to the tip, then drove into her wet, tight heat. Every moan vibrating against his ear, every almost scream drove him on deeper, harder. "Christ, Mary. I don't want to hurt you. Tell me to stop."

"If. You. Stop. I will kill you," she gasped.

He chuckled. "Not dying today, sweetheart." Not until he'd committed to memory every gasp, groan and kiss.

He cupped her breast and squeezed her deep red nipple between his fingers, pinched it hard and sucked it into his mouth.

"Yes. More."

He slid his mouth across her cheek to the pulse point on her neck. Biting and sucking, rocking inside her. She tasted sweet with a hint of tartness that never failed to drive him wild.

Her legs tightened around his waist. Sucking him deeper, she rocked her hips back and forth, speeding up the rhythm. He wasn't sure how long he'd last before he flew over the edge.

He slid his hand between their bodies and pinched her clit. Her curse made him smile. Heart pounding, he stroked the pad of his thumb over her nub and the moment her breath caught, he pressed his thumb to his finger.

"Yes. Like that." Her breath caught in her chest and her eyes closed.

So fucking beautiful. "Breathe. Look at me." *Say my name.*

If this was the one and only time he got to be inside her, he wanted to hear her scream it. A memory to hold on to when his nights returned to being dark and long.

He thrust one more time and held still. Her eyes fluttered open. She was doing her best to make it last, but with every hitch of her breath, she came closer to the edge. "Look at me when you come."

Moving again, he picked up the pace, short and fast until he felt his balls pull tight and the tingle at the base of spine. Once more, then he pinched her clit, harder this time, and they fell together.

Yelling her name as he came, He poured everything he was into her and lost himself in a shit ton of feelings he should have let lie. Their breaths crashing against one another until they disappeared into the calm.

"I love you," she whispered.

Fuck knew, he wanted to say same. Every inch of him felt it. Instead, he eased his weight onto his elbows and kissed her. They had a lot to work through, but there was no fucking doubt in his mind this is where Mary Maud Lane belonged. Nestled against his chest. Her ear resting on his heart.

Chapter Twenty-Three

THE MAN WAS TRAINED. He had been sitting there all night watching the house. No set routine, random timing accompanied his perimeter checks. But aware or not, the guy had a rhythm. Once started, the circuit was long enough for him to get what he needed from the sister and disappear.

He straightened his tie, cleared his throat and pressed the doorbell. Seconds later, the chime still pulsed in the air when Sara Lane answered the door. Mary's sister cocked her head to one side and waited for him to speak.

Ten pounds heavier, she looked nothing like her sibling. Dressed in jeans and a Berkley sweatshirt, her hair sat in a neat bun on top of her head. It lacked her sister's shine. Her eyes were steel-cold blue. Mary's eyes shone with the color of the Pacific Ocean on a warm summer's day.

"Who are you? What do you want?" She bristled.

I'm the serial killer from next door. Big bad wolf had a nice ring to it, but he bit his tongue and didn't answer straight away, not until she held her breath and leaned her weight against the door. "Sara Lane?" He flashed his badge.

"Yes?"

"U.S. Marshal. Can I come in? I'd like to speak to your sister. Is she in?"

The door jittered as she squinted at the I.D. retreating into his pocket.

"Anyway. She's not here." And how do I know that's not fake?"

Nodding, he stepped back. "Your sister has a daughter, Lucy. She's five, loves her bunny, Floppy Hop. Can't sleep without it." The sister's shoulders relaxed. *You're winning.* "Mary has a limp. Not the result of falling off the roundabout as a kid." Willing curiosity to win her over, he paused. "Do you know where I can reach her?"

"You'd better come in. Can I get you a coffee? I was just about to make one."

"Coffee sounds great, but no can do. I apologize for showing up out of the blue like this. I should have called."

"Well, I'm sorry I can't help you...

"Are you sure? Technically, I shouldn't be here, but I'm worried about Ms. Lane." He loosened his tie a fraction, watching her curiosity spike. "Ms. Lane broke protocol and left our protection. Boss wants me to close the file." He raised an eyebrow.

"But?"

Hooked. "I was her handler for over five years, Sara. Apologies. May I call you, Sara?"

"I guess so."

"Well, Sara. I'm Frank, by the way. We're not supposed to get close, but six years is a long time. You kinda get to know someone, and I just want to know she and cute kid are safe." He smiled and lowered his gaze. "Vokov, the criminal she was helping us convict, escaped. I want to help them." Looking straight at her now, he gave her space to speak.

"Mary doesn't need your help. She has, Matt."

"Matt?"

"Look. I'm sorry, but I have to get to work." The skin underneath her eye twitched.

"Understand. I'll let you go. Good to know she has someone looking out for her. Matt. He's your brother, right?" *Like hell.*

"No. Her fiancé, ex-fiancé. He works for a big security company in Manhattan. I'm surprised she didn't tell you."

He angled his body toward the steps. "Yeah, yeah. It's coming back to me. Guess I should have taken you up on the offer of that coffee.

I'd like to team up with Matt. Work together to protect Ms. Lane and Lucy. Sure, you don't know where they went?" Sis was a tough nut to crack. "Hey, I almost forgot. Maybe you'd like these?"

He reached in his pocket for the backup photos he'd brought, just in case. They spanned the missing years. Guaranteed tear jerkers. He added a quick description of Lucy's first day at kindergarten, and sis forgot she had a job.

"I should have been there," she whispered.

"Make it right, Sara. Tell me where your sister is."

Whether it was the way he said her name, or the relief of sharing her thoughts with someone she felt understood, he didn't care. She caved.

"Matt has a cabin. Upstate, New York, near Rochester. He didn't tell me the exact location. Maybe his friend, Dex, knows?" Sara peered over his shoulder. "He should be back any minute."

"Hey. Relax. You've been a great help." He patted her hand. "I'll find them and make sure they're safe until Vokov is caught."

"Thank you. When you see her. Tell her..."

"Anything."

"Nothing. Give Lucy a hug for me."

Promising to call with updates, he left. As she watched him drive off, he forced a smile and a wave. A fuck ton of crap there. *Families.*

Now was as good a time as any to call Vokov, so he hit his number and braced for his lover's familiar snarl.

"Well?" Vokov's accent was thicker at night.

"The bodyguard, Matt, her ex, it turns out, has taken Mary and the kid to his cabin upstate. They have history."

"So, why are you calling me? You're on your way there. Yes?"

Frank's grip tightened on the phone. "This is a bad idea. This guy is the fiancé she left behind when she entered WITSEC. On top of his vested interest, he and the others at Sentinel are highly trained, ex special forces. Lay down his life, hero shit."

"And? You have a problem with that?" Vokov snapped. "I'd have thought you'd enjoy helping him on his way."

Frank was tired of this crap. If the man wasn't so goddam good at fucking his ass, he'd have left him long ago. "Perhaps I don't feel like finding out. Losing your brother, I get it, but trust me, go after her and this will end badly."

"You think I care about the risk?"

"Easy for you, *myshka*. It's me freezing my balls off out here."

"The bitch killed Maxim. She must pay."

Frank clenched the steering wheel. "If your goddam brother hadn't been such a goddam idiot, and tried to kidnap a girl in broad daylight, the cops may not have shot him. Sad fact, but this is on him, not the woman." *Or her five-year-old daughter.*

"Tut, tut, are you going soft on me? If you cannot live up to expectations, I need someone new in my life. Someone with balls."

"My balls are plenty big enough for you to handle when we're..."

"Do not push me," Vokov interrupted. "I'd hate to see you end up like Mr. Tumbler, *drogoya*."

"Put your dick back in your pants, lover, before this someone chops it off." Two could play cock on top. "You're losing sight of the bigger picture."

"Do your job. It would break my heart to lose you." Vokov sneered.

"And if I don't? What will you..."

Vokov's laugh cut him off. "Then you'll wish you had."

Frank took a deep breath. "This will destroy you."

"Let me be clear. I do not need saving. Bring her and her daughter to me."

"Then what? You plan on killing a kid?" He pressed on, knowing the fucking answer.

"What do they say in your country? Collateral damage?"

"Try life without parole. Besides, I kinda draw the line at murder under the age of seven."

"As you wish, my friend. I will find them, with or without you. I'd say, have a nice day, but we both know that's no longer possible."

Bile rose to the back of Frank's throat. "Fuck you, asshole." He tossed his phone onto the passenger seat, opened the car door and spat onto the street.

Chapter Twenty-Four

Holding hands, watching the sun rise and fall. No, he had never been big on the romantic stuff women held out for. But the universe might call him a liar. Especially if it saw him watching this morning's first light creep through the curtains and fall on Mary's skin. The sight robbed him of breath, scared the hell out of him, as words, more for a poet, like translucent, ethereal, floated over his lips.

The sweet smell of her skin melded with the musky scent of their lovemaking, and for a dumb moment, Trig imagined waking up every day lying next to her, Lucy asleep down the hall. *Get a fucking grip.*

He had woken up, muscles tense, ready to spring into action at the feel of the unfamiliar weight pressed to his chest, until he remembered making love to Mary, the only woman who had ever spent the entire night in his bed.

Years serving in the military, and now with Sentinel, meant he never stepped into danger unless he was armed to the fucking teeth. So why had he surrendered to Mary Maud Lane? He wasn't ready to tell her, but deep in his gut he knew if she ran from him again, he wouldn't survive.

A family, this family, lazy Sunday mornings, bedtime stories, sugar, and spice and all things fuck ton impossible was never meant for him.

At the sound of bird feet scratching the tin roof, Mary stirred. His cock sprung to attention at her long, sleepy sigh. Prepared for action. Except, he wasn't ready to face her, to navigate the minefield of emotions roaring inside him.

Besides, he promised to call Snake, so he slipped from under the covers, pulled on his pants and dragged his tee over his head. He made it to the front door before Lucy cried out. His feet did a swift detour.

Sitting up in bed, Floppy Hop clutched to her chest, the kid rubbed the sleep out of her eyes.

"Hug," she said, her bottom lip curling.

Heart cracking, he sat beside her, pulled her into his arms, and kissed her cheek. *Feels so fucking right. But she can't be yours.* "Good morning, poppet."

Lucy tilted her head to one side. Eyes bluer than her mother's, if that were possible, peered at him from under the longest lashes he'd ever seen.

"You and Mommy friends?"

Her innocent question threw him. "It's... complicated, sweetheart," he managed. *Complicated? She's five. Jeez.*

"Are you mad at her?" Lucy pressed.

Trigger sighed and ran the edge of his pinky over her cheek. "No, poppet. But you and your mom are leaving soon," he blurted as if that answered her question.

"Why?" Lucy pouted.

Adorable.

"I want to stay with you."

"I know. But it's not possible." Behind him, the damn floorboards creaked, followed by Mary's soft gasp. She stood in the doorway, eyes filled with hurt. *Me and my dumb mouth.*

Short of cutting off his tongue, he should have explained. At least assured them he intended to spend the rest of his life making sure they were safe.

Even as his heart screamed, go to her, his hands curled into fists, and he kept his damn mouth shut. Easier. Safer.

"Story, Trigger?"

Lucy bounced on the bed, the drama between him and her mom soaring over her head. Moving on, Lucy's tiny fingers reached for the book beside the bed. "Sure, poppet." He scooted her backside on to his knee. "After this, we can go for breakfast, pick up supplies," he yelled at Mary's retreating back.

"Whatever."

Yeah, pissed, worse, disappointed. Big mistake not following her. His head got it. Pity the rest of him refused to catch up.

***

Thanks to the dumping of snow last night, Matt took his time navigating the narrow road. Mary stared out the window, her breath fogging the glass as she watched the snow-covered world glide by. In the back seat, Lucy hummed one of her favorite nursery rhymes.

He had chosen a beautiful spot to build. Peaceful, a quiet that wrapped around your heart. She'd been right yesterday about hearing water. A small creek snaked its way through the trees. Unfortunately, the beauty didn't soften the impact of Matt's words.

A man who found it hard to let the past go anchored his gaze on the road in front of him as though their destination held the answer to the mysteries of the universe. Not the two people in the car with him, wishing like hell they could get through the pain and move forward together.

Last night they'd made love like they did when they first met. Passionate, playful, like the two people they used to be. Lovers who swore a lifetime together was too short. Yes, she'd messed up big time, but in her dreams, she allowed herself to believe they might finally be a family. But she'd heard it with her own ears. He planned on leaving them.

No use crying. Being alone was nothing new. Her fear was for Lucy. Not knowing a parent's love left a damn big hole. Forcing a smile, she turned to face her daughter, who was fascinated by the snowflakes nose diving across her window. Boxed in, her heart beat faster. Taking a deep breath impossible. Thank God the local gas station appeared up ahead. Beside it, the café and store.

"Pancakes!" Lucy clapped her hands as they pulled into the parking lot.

Matt opened his door and went around to lift her out and onto his shoulders. "Hands round my neck. Don't want your feet to get wet."

"Look, mommy. I'm flying."

"Uh, huh." The smell of coffee and maple syrup wafting from the café wrapped her in a welcome comfort blanket. They settled into a booth by the window, Lucy between them, creating a buffer.

"Trigger. Haven't seen you in these parts for some time. What can I get you folks?" The cheerful waitress winked at Lucy.

"Chocolate chip pancakes." Lucy declared and crossed her chubby arms.

"That's a lot of sugar, sweetheart." *Seriously?* She deserved a lifetime of whatever she wanted.

"I'll have the same." Matt glanced at her. "Your favorite still blueberry?"

Christ, the fact he remembered ignited a flame under the pile of wishes and wants that were never going to happen. "Yes. Thanks. And a coffee."

As they waited for their food, Lucy filled the time telling them about last night's dream. Talking animals and magical snowmen. Genuinely interested, Matt's focus didn't leave his daughter's face. Damn this crap. She needed to kiss him. More, and if Lucy wasn't sitting between them, she'd have reached under the table and...

Saved by the pancakes. They looked delicious, but the knot in her stomach made it impossible to do more than pick.

"Taste mine," Matt said, holding his fork to her mouth.

"Silly. They're the same," Lucy giggled.

"Nope."

Her child's eyes almost popped out of her head when he swallowed the bite on her fork.

"Ah ha. Mine are way better."

As they ate breakfast, Matt continued to entertain them. At one point, she called for sixty seconds of silence just so Lucy could stop laughing long enough to drink her juice. This was the family they could be, if only he'd let them in.

"Okay, if you're done." Matt glanced at her half-eaten food.

"I am." She glanced at her kid's bulging cheeks and smiled. "Swallow, sweetie." Matt waited for Lucy to finish and tossed several bills onto the table.

"Catch you later, Jenny. C'mon, we need to pick up supplies before the road turns icy," he said.

Next door, she moved through the small store, on autopilot, grabbing essentials while Matt and Lucy took off to find dinner.

The trip back seemed to go a lot faster. Thanks to Lucy insisting on a game of I Spy. Thrilled at the untouched snow surrounding the cabin, Lucy begged Matt to play with her outside.

Grateful for time alone, she stayed inside, putting away groceries and pulling herself together. Through the kitchen window, she watched them build a snowman. Lucy's delighted squeals drifting inside the cabin as Matt rolled a large ball for the body.

Dropping to his knees, he helped her find some stones for his eyes. His deep laugh echoing through the trees as Lucy plopped a handful of snow on top of his head.

Mad at herself for wishing things were different, she reached for the dish towel and dabbed at her tears. Matt glanced over his shoulder in her direction. *Oh, hell.* "Onions," she mouthed and waved.

Chapter Twenty-Five

Mary sat in the Adirondack, savoring the smell of the meat grilling over the fire. Matt insisted his secret marinade of aromatic spices was magic to die for. Every time he flipped one of the giant burgers, the muscles of his forearms rippled, and a satisfied grin played on his lips.

But that wasn't the only thing that made her mouth water. His promise to top them with melted cheese, bacon, and a tangy aioli had her drooling.

That afternoon, while she and Lucy spent time coloring, he had disappeared. Not too far away, she suspected, but he didn't return until it was time to start the fire.

"Dinner is served, my lady." Matt placed the overstuffed plate of food on the log in front of them and lowered his powerful body into the chair beside her.

"Up." Lucy stretched her arms above her head.

"Easy there, poppet." He scooped her onto his knee. "Here you go." He winked.

The kid's eyes popped when he handed her a burger that dwarfed her small hands. Even with her mouth open wide, the juice oozed over the poor kid's chin.

Mary chuckled. "Remember, sweetheart, little people bites. Here, let me cut them."

Matt's eyes twinkled with mischief.

"Like this, poppet," he picked up his burger, hunched his shoulders, and grunted. Lucy squealed as he dived in for an enormous, messy mouthful, and licked the sauce from his cheeks.

"Fine example you are." Mary smiled, recalling how that talented tongue had brought her to orgasm many times. The spot below her navel tingled.

"You, too, mommy. Take a Gawilla bite."

"Okay." With a grunt, not nearly as impressive as Matt's, she chomped into the scrumptious burger.

Matt reached across and swiped the aioli from the side of her mouth with the pad of his thumb. "Delicious."

Good job their daughter already occupied the prime spot, otherwise she might have been tempted to hop over the arm of her chair and get comfortable in his lap.

"Here you go, poppet."

Matt cut the burger into quarters and handed their daughter a smaller portion.

"Baby Gawilla bites." She beamed.

Too much. How the hell was she going to keep pulling up her big girl panties, accepting they didn't have long together when Matt didn't play fair? A tear rushed to the corner of her eye, and the growing tightness in her chest threatened to suffocate her. She groaned.

"Mommy?" Lucy frowned.

"S'okay, sweetie. Mommy will be back in a sec. Eat your burger before it gets cold." Before she made a complete idiot of herself, she rushed inside and locked herself in the bathroom.

A part of her wished Matt had followed, cupped her cheeks, kissed her, told her he forgave her, and that everything would be okay. *Not happening.* Hiding in the bathroom was childish. Grabbing the facecloth, she ran it under the cold water and slapped it onto her face. The sudden chill made her gasp. *Better.*

She hadn't been gone long, but by the time she rejoined by the fire, the evening had turned colder. "Bedtime, sweetie." Mary started gathering the dirty plates.

In one fluid motion, daughter in his arms, Matt rose from his chair. "Leave those. I'll take care of them."

"Uh, huh. You cooked. I'll wash the dishes." Fair and keeping her hands busy with something other than stroking his body was a good thing. Right?

Lucy pouted. "I want to play a game. Please," she added.

Matt kissed her cheek. "How about it, mommy? *Please.*"

Mary didn't stand a chance. One glimpse of his honey brown eyes, peering over the top of Lucy's head, and she was all in. "Okay, you guys, one game, then bed, Miss Lucy."

"Promise." Lucy's gaze landed on Matt. "I Spy?" she asked.

"Again? Okay, but this time I win." He raised his free arm and flexed his biceps.

"Silly." Lucy giggled.

"Me first," she squealed as her porter bounced her on the couch.

"How about we let mommy go first, poppet?"

"Okay, but not too hard, mommy."

"I think I can manage that. Um. I spy, with my little eye, something beginning with F."

"That's too easy. Fire." Lucy clapped. "My turn. I spy with my little eye something beginning with S B."

Matt frowned, sat on the couch, and settled Lucy on his knee. *Welcome to the game.* After several guesses, she gave up, but bull headed, he kept guessing.

"Do you give up?" Lucy sighed.

"Okay. You got me," he said, looking like he wasn't used to surrender.

"Sad Bear," Lucy announced, and buried her tiny finger in his massive chest.

A lump the size of Mount Etna lodged in Mary's throat.

"I won. Me, again."

For the next half hour, their daughter ran rings around them, until her head fell against Matt's chest, a huge yawn catching her breath.

"Sleepy," Lucy mumbled. "Story."

"Okay, poppet."

"Cuddle time." Lucy wrapped her arm around Matt's neck and wiggled her fingers. "Come closer, mommy."

"Okay, I'm coming." Mary trailed after them, not sure if she could keep from balling. "How about we hug hands tonight, sweetie?" She grabbed one, and Matt took his cue, snagging the other, as he settled Lucy on the bed, and they sat on either side of her.

"Once upon a time." he cleared his throat, looking as though he wasn't sure that was how to start. "In a land far away, there lived this knight named Sir Squish-a-lot," Matt began.

Oh yeah. You got this.

"He wasn't the biggest or strongest knight, but he had the bravest heart, and the Princess loved him. One day, a dragon came to the castle. He breathed fire and scared everyone. All the big knights ran away, but not Sir Squish-a-lot. He wanted to keep his princess safe, so he walked right up to the dragon and said, 'Mr. Dragon, why are you so angry?' And guess what? It turned out the dragon had a tummy ache from eating too many burgers!"

Lucy giggled. "Too many gawilla bites, mommy."

"For sure. So, what did Sir Squish-a-lot do next?" Mary asked.

"Er. He gave the dragon some tummy medicine, and they became best friends." His voice trailed away.

The soft brush of his lips against her child's hair made her heart swell. She would love this man until the day she died. At least.

After pulling the covers up under Lucy's chin, making sure she was snuggled in nice and tight, they crept out of the room, Matt's arm around her shoulder, his expression warm, soft.

"You should get some rest, too," he said.

His hand shifted to her lower back and guided her out of Lucy's room and into his bedroom. Remembering the last time he'd shown interest in her sleep patterns, she stopped walking and smiled. "I suppose so. Care to join me?"

Thinking she'd have at least a breath to realize what she'd offered; she was equal parts shocked and elated when he cupped her face in his hands and kissed her. The take-all plundering she expected and craved every waking moment.

When they broke apart seconds later, she searched his eyes for a sign that everything between them was okay. Or was his forehead pressed against hers, his thumb caressing the tip of her chin, the start of a bittersweet goodbye?

"Make love to me, Matt." Her hand trembling, she brushed her fingers along the scar Lucy had noticed earlier. The look in his eyes when she'd called out his owie had been one of surprise. Men like him took every blow tossed at them and carried on, just as he had when she disappeared.

"Sleep is overrated," he groaned, circling her waist with both hands and pulling her flush against him.

Matt's mouth claimed hers, demanding she surrender any lingering doubt in her mind that this was a good idea. Her body relaxed under the soothing glide of his hands over her hips, and her sex softened against his erection.

Mary wrenched her mouth free, sure she should say something more, but she couldn't think the hell it might be, so she gasped, drawing in a deep breath and joined him in another earth-shattering kiss.

His brown eyes turned black with a desire that flirted with her own. Pure, masculine energy that screamed through every inch of him she was his, and there was no way he'd let her go again.

Christ, she wanted it to be true. Her whole body trembled with the raw need to give herself to him. Completely. Forever.

"I love you, Mary." Matt nibbled her bottom lip. "I never stopped."

"I love you, too. There has never been anyone else for me. You're it, lover." He leaned in, hoping they'd stay like that, kissing away every scar left by the past six years, but he took a step back.

No. Before any lingering insecurity ruined what promised to grow between them, he scooped her into his arms and laid her on the bed. Careful not to land heavily on top of her, he lowered his body onto his elbows and stretched over her.

Her hips writhed against his pelvis. If she didn't have him inside her in the next ten seconds, she'd self combust. "Matt."

"Shh."

His mouth pressed against her neck and trailed a line of kisses over her still clothed body. *Damn.* "Need to get naked," she whispered, tugging at the waistband of her jeans.

"Easy. What's your rush?"

She felt his smile curve against her jaw as he sucked on her earlobe. Delicious. There was no other word to describe the tremors rippling through her torso, the bright tingling between her thighs.

"I'm close, baby," she gasped, trying to hold on to what felt like a tsunami washing through her.

Matt grinned. "You are the most beautiful woman I have ever seen. Be my guest."

And just like that, her breath caught in her chest. He licked the space between her breasts, his day old stubble scratching her skin.

"Oh, God," she whimpered, and shoved her hand under her waistband and into her panties.

"Uh, huh! Mine," he said and replaced her fingers with his.

The pinch made her squeal and then she was falling, her breath finally free to gasp his name. Content to lie there as he removed her clothes, the loneliness of the past disappeared in a satiated haze.

Returning the favor, she undid the button of his pants and tugged them over his hips. Matt moved with masculine grace, leveraging himself onto one knee and off the bed. Shucking his jeans and underwear in one move, the tee came next, revealing muscles that rippled. Or maybe that was just the lust fueled haze across her vision?

"What's so funny?" he asked, climbing back onto the bed and stroking a strand of hair from the corner of her mouth.

"This. You. Me. Hell, I'm not sure. I'm happy." She watched his eyes close for a sec, and then he nodded.

"I'm glad. All I ever wanted was for you to be happy. To keep you safe."

"I know. Now kiss me," she said, not wanting to go backwards. "Kiss me. Or do I have to beg?"

"Never."

His mouth covered her nipple, the nip of his teeth sending electric shocks through her entire body. Tugging on his short hair, she moaned and lifted her hips to meet his. "Matt. I..."

"Breathe, sweetheart."

Matt took her hand and traced it down his torso. The feel of his solid muscles braced against her fingertips was amazing. He didn't let go until her fingers curled around his swollen shaft.

"Feel how much I miss you?" he said, his voice hoarse.

"I do." She let her legs fall apart. "Come inside."

"Damn. Protection, it's in my bag."

"It's okay. I'm on the pill."

"And I'm clean, sweetheart. You're sure?"

His low groan was satisfying, knowing he was as desperate as she was to feel him moving inside her. Inch by torturous inch, he eased inside her, taking his time to give her exactly what she craved. Fully seated, he stopped moving.

"More," she thumped his back.

"Like this?" He drew back and thrust hard and deep, hitting places she never dreamed existed.

"Yes." How could she be this close so soon? "Keep moving," she cried out as he set a pace that made the tips of her ears burn and his fingers found her clit. "You are killing me, Matt. It's been a long time.

He stilled. "Am I hurting you?"

"Hell, no."

His nose nuzzled her ear. "Good." Slipping one hand under her hips, he pulled her closer and changed the angle of his thrust.

"I'm close, sweetheart." Matt pressed harder on her clit and increased his pace.

Her body started to shake.

"So good. That's it. Come with me, baby." His breath hitched.

"Matt!" she panted as the feel of their bodies moving as one, the rough edge of his finger rubbing her clit, sent her headlong into oblivion.

His mouth swallowed her scream before one last thrust and his semen flooded her womb. "Oh, my God," she murmured over their loud pants.

"If you say so." His palm brushed the side of her cheek.

"Idiot."

"Yes, ma'am, but I'm your idiot."

Mary lifted her head, meeting his gaze. The vulnerability in his eyes made her heart swell. "You're it for me, Matt."

Chapter Twenty-Six

Trig lay in the dark, his body relaxed and satiated. His girl, Mary, the only woman who had that power to wring him out and leave him craving more of her touch, her kiss in his bed. Everything she gifted him. *Fucking perfect.*

So, what was that damn noise? Why were the sheets cold?

He reached for a feel of her naked body. The sheets were cold. He stretched further, his blood turning to ice. *Your bed is big dickhead. Not that fucking big.*

Gone. No way. He needed her here, right the hell now. Head pounding, he scrubbed his fingers over his scalp and listened for any out-of-place murmur. Poor kid was sleeping too great. He rolled out of bed to see if he could help. A smile tugged at his mouth. She liked his stories.

The scream came from nowhere. Too loud for Lucy. Mary? Pulling on his jeans, he claimed his Glock from the drawer. Still dark, just passed three, according to the luminous hands on the battery-operated clock.

Lower your weapon. There was a kid in the house. Taking a deep breath, he ran likely scenarios and decided Lucy had a nightmare. Mary went to check on her.

Curling his fingers around his weapon, he kept by his side as he crept to the guest bedroom. Lucy hadn't stirred. Thank God when the kid did sleep, she was out for the count. No sign of her mom. The realization hit as a second scream shattered the night.

Closing the door behind him. Crouching to avoid the windows, head on a swivel, he moved like a ghost through the cabin. The light on the security panel flashed red. Disarmed. *No way.*

Adrenaline pumped through his body. Back to the wall, he sniffed in a breath and steadied his pulse. Years of special ops training taught him how to channel his fear and focus.

He swung across to the narrow window beside the front door and pushed aside the blind with the tip of his finger. Dressed in yoga pants and a long-sleeve tee, Mary struggled with a man dressed in black wearing a balaclava. The bastard had her in a chokehold, a pistol pressed to her temple.

Clasping his weapon in both hands, he opened the door and stepped onto the porch. "Let her go," he commanded. He kept his voice low. Unless the guy was a complete moron, there was no mistaking the lethal threat in his tone. "Look at me, sweetheart. Everything's okay."

Mary's jaw dropped. Fair. They had a few seconds to go before he blew this fucker's head off, but she should trust him to keep her safe.

"Back off, hero, or I paint the ground with your girl's brains."

The fucker tightened his grip on her throat. "Not happening, dickwad. Release her and drive away if you want to live."

"Yeah. Like you'd risk it." The man laughed.

Valid point, but then he didn't know who he was dealing with, what he was capable of doing. Trig fired. Tap. Tap. The bullets blasted through the balaclava and buried themselves in his skull. *That's the way to do it.* The intruder crumpled, dragging Mary to the ground with him before his arm lost their grip.

"Christ!" Clawing at her blood-stained tee, Mary scrambled away from the body.

Seizing her elbow, he pulled her to her feet. "Inside. Now! Lock the door. Stay with Lucy."

"No. Don't leave, Matt." Her voice shook.

Hell, he wanted to stay, shelter her from the nightmares glistening in her blue eyes, but he had to make sure there were no intruders lurking beyond the tree line. "I'll be back. Go."

After he heard the familiar beep of the security system, he climbed to higher ground for a stronger signal and called Snake.

"Hadn't expected to hear from you 'til morning." Snake huffed.

Obviously, the boss had some sort of timetable in his head for these check-ins that he hadn't figured out. *Tough.* "We have a situation at the cabin. Some mother fucker had a gun to Mary's head."

"He's dead." Snake confirmed.

"Roger that." The boss should be chewing his ear off for letting it happen. "Need cleanup assist. Winter available?"

"On his way."

"This place is off grid. How the hell did they track us?" Only Sentinel and Sara knew the direction they headed after leaving her place. He trusted his brothers with his life, and despite the sisterly love fubar, he didn't rate Sara giving up her sister to a murdering child trafficker.

"Million-dollar question. Hawke's on it. Watch your six."

Trigger ended the call, his head telling him to sweep of the perimeter again, but he needed to make sure Mary and Lucy were okay first. Moving quickly, he headed back to the cabin.

As soon as he walked through the door, she jumped from the couch and flew into his arms. *Where you belong.* Dirt and tears streaked her terrified face. And he wanted to fucking strangle her. "Why the hell did you go outside?" he demanded. "You trying to get yourself killed? Coz, it can be arranged."

"Don't be an idiot," she huffed. "I couldn't sleep, and I didn't want to wake you. I went onto the porch to call Sara and make sure she was okay."

"Are you fucking kidding me? After everything? The warnings, the attempts on your life. What part of, I'm here to protect you, works with me getting a good night's sleep?"

"I'm sick of living like this, Matt, jumping at shadows. Trapped."

"You might not live at all if you pull another stunt like that!" His breath caught at the sight of her tears. "Oh, sweetheart. Come here." Taking her into his arms, he tugged her close, his mouth grazing her lips. The same peace he felt when they made love flowed from the fingers gripping his arm.

"Mommy?"

As one, they swiveled to face the small voice. Lucy stood in the doorway, Floppy Hop clutched to her chest, her tiny fist rubbing her eyes.

"I'm here, sweetie." Mary kneeled beside her and gave her a hug.

"Why are you crying?" Lucy asked. "Are you fighting?" She lowered her chin and glared at him.

Mary sighed. "No, baby. I've got something in my eye."

"I want a story," Lucy mumbled, half-asleep.

"Sure thing. First, let's get you back to bed."

After what she'd just been through, she still managed to smile at her daughter. *Goddamit.* Why did this woman, his woman, have to be so fucking beautiful?

When he went to pick the kid up, Mary glared at him. *Not invited.* He shouldn't have yelled at her, but when he saw her with a gun to her head, he almost lost his mind. What if he hadn't got to her in time? He wouldn't survive losing her again.

Anger and fear battled for line honors inside him. He needed air. Had to hide the body until Winter arrived and took care of it. Another dumb move on his part. Dead men didn't talk.

Trigger approached the body. No way did the guy have a pulse, but he kept his weapon aimed at his head. With his free hand, he stripped off the balaclava. No distinguishing marks or features, but Hawke could run prints, check for a DNA match.

No phone, no wallet. No keys. *How the hell did you get here?* At the rustling in the trees, he crouched and raised his weapon. Sucking in a breath, he watched the animal, curious about the fuss, blink and disappear.

No threat. This time. But out there somewhere, Vokov was plotting his next move. Trig straightened his spine. "Bring it, mother fucker, I'm waiting."

Chapter Twenty-Seven

Hawke flicked a purple-streaked strand of hair across her face and out of her eyes. Peering through her glasses at the scrolling lines of code on her screen, she added to things to her mental to-do list. Get a haircut and fix her squeaky chair to her mental to-do list.

Her tech cave hummed with servers and cooling fans. Three curved 40-inch monitors dominated one wall, while smaller displays showed different security feeds, data streams, and tracking programs.

Empty energy drink cans stacked up beside her wireless charging pad resembled a mini cityscape. "Come on, you sneaky bastard." She'd been at this for thirty-six hours straight. Giving up was not an option.

Finding Mary's mole was personal. Someone had compromised her safe location. Twice, for fuck's sake, putting not only her at risk, but Lucy too. A five-year-old. Who did that shit?

In front of her, the AI-driven correlation program chirped, highlighting another data anomaly. False lead number seventeen. Hawke grabbed the armrests of her ergonomic gaming chair. Essential in her line of work. She spent too much time sitting. It was a miracle her ass wasn't stuck to it.

Stretching her legs under her desk, she straightened her spine and cracked her neck a couple of times. A move guaranteed to give her an energy spurt unless she needed brain food. Genius Juice, the guys called it. The secret recipe transported her outside the box when conventional hacking failed.

Prying herself from her chair, she pulled frozen strawberries and almond milk from her mini-fridge and snatched her favorite anime glass from the shelf. Into the blender, she dropped vanilla protein powder, scoops of chocolate ice cream, and flicked the switch.

During the day, she drank coffee, gallons of it, but sometimes in the dead of night, when the tech goddess had forsaken her, the cold, sugary drink hit the spot.

Something on Monitor Two caught her eye, a pattern in the data she hadn't noticed before. Genius juice in hand, she returned to her station. "Well, hello there," she whispered, setting down her shake, and resuming her finger dance across the keyboard. "What are you hiding?"

The program she'd written to track digital footprints flagged a series of encrypted communications. On their own, nothing suspicious, except for the timing. Each transmission occurred consistently prior to a leak about Mary's location.

"Gotcha by the ones and zeros," Hawke grinned, and began unraveling the encryption, her custom software peeling back digital onion layers of security.

The first, standard government protocol.

The second, U.S. Marshal service specific.

"No fucking way," Hawke cursed, spinning in her chair. "Give me more, goddess," she muttered, and deployed her favorite program, SHERLOCK (Systematic Heuristic Extraction and Reconnaissance Locating Obscured Connections Kernel).

SHERLOCK pulled everything. Phone records, financial transactions, travel patterns, surveillance footage. In front of her, streaming across her screen, the bot compiled and correlated, building data until... *You are shitting me.* The fog cleared, revealing the thread connecting the pieces she'd been missing, and the third layer cracked.

US Marshal Frank Donovan. Her pulse quickened. Mary's handler during the WITSEC program, a man who'd been there when she was at her most vulnerable. The creep she trusted.

Hawke pulled up a fresh set of data logs. Embedded in encrypted communication channels, she found the marshal's name.

Timestamps, precise moments, recorded every time they confirmed Mary's safe location.

"Holy mother of geeks." Clear as daylight on her center screen, up popped surveillance photos from a hotel three months ago. Donovan entering the elevator, Vokov standing behind him.

More images, the two of them taking in the sun at a villa in Montenegro. Wire transfers from a shell company linking to the criminal's organization to an offshore account in Donovan's name. And, hey presto, intimate text messages between the two men. *You can't help who you fall in lust with.*

"Got ya." Hawke reached for her phone and called Snake.

"Talk to me."

"Found our mole." Still staring at the evidence, Hawke preened. "You're not gonna believe it."

"Try me."

"It's Donovan."

Silence. Then, "Say again."

"US Marshal Frank Donovan has been feeding Vokov information about Mary's locations, the cabin, every goddam move she makes. Looks like the two are fucking."

"Son of a bitch." Snake's voice was deadly quiet. "You're sure?"

"You know me better than that. I don't make this shit up." Hawke said, kind of hurt he doubted her.

Another long pause. Boss man, tensing his jaw, processing the intel, she guessed. "I've got enough evidence to bury him. Photos, messages, money transfers. Sick fuck."

"Send everything to me and the relevant agencies. Call Tri and let him know I'll have a team mobilized to his location within the hour."

"On it. Already compiling the file, and I'll call him now."

She waited for the click and dialed Trig.

"Hawke? What's happening, my friend?"

"Is Mary with you?"

"Yeah, she just walked in. Hold on." Trigger's voice became muffled. "Sit down, sweetheart. Hawke has news."

Hawke stared at the damning evidence of Donovan's betrayal on her screen while she relayed the facts. Trig's string of loud curses forced the phone from her ear.

"No, that's impossible. Frank's my friend. He protected us, helped me," Mary protested in the background.

"While feeding information to his lover," Trigger said, keeping his voice low. "You heard Hawke, sweetheart. She has proof Donovan and Vokov were together before you entered witness protection."

"I trusted him. Lucy adores him."

Hawke took a gulp of her genius juice. Shit was getting heavy and dealing with emotional crap was not her strong suit. Not that she didn't care but give her machines any day. "I'm sending everything through to you and the boss. He also wants it sent to the FBI." Hawke interjected. "He said to let you know he's sending backup your way. Heading to you within the hour."

"No. I don't believe it."

Trig's woman was digging in.

Mary groaned. "I told you, Matt. I am done hiding. Done letting these people control my life. We're going back to Manhattan."

You go, girl.

"Be reasonable, sweetheart," Trigger grumbled.

"I mean it, Trig. I won't raise Lucy like this, jumping at shadows, never knowing who to trust. We face Vokov head on. End this."

Before she let them go, Hawke pulled up the satellite imagery of Trig's building. "Hey, guys, sorry to interrupt. Trig, I checked, and I can have security protocols at your place upgraded within twenty-four hours. Triple authentication, biometric scanners, the works." She rubbed her hands together.

"Do it," he ordered. "Great work, Hawke."

"Aww. Feeling the fuzzy-wuzzies, big guy. Thanks. But it's what I do. Nosy nerd with too many computers." She cracked her knuckles, already plotting the additional security measures. "I'll continue digging, see what else I can find on Donovan and Vokov."

"Yes. Thanks Hawke. I'd love to finally meet you. I'll buy you dinner." Mary added.

"I'll hold you to it." She smiled and hung up. A woman who thought of food when her head was on the chopping block sounded like the kind of gal she would be happy to get to know better.

Leaning against the back of her chair, she slurped the last of the melted ice-cream through the straw. On her main screen, SHER-

LOCK continued analyzing data, building the web of connections. A photo of Donovan and Vokov filled one monitor. The Russian's arm curled possessively round the marshal's waist as they smiled at a private joke.

"Game over, boys." As the boss ordered, she sent off her findings. The last one heading to the FBI. "Nobody messes with the Sentinel family."

She pulled up the schematics for Trig's apartment. If they were coming home, she'd make damn sure it was the safest place in the universe.

As she settled in for a long night, the cave buzzed around her, servers processing, programs running. Sometimes the best weapon wasn't a gun or a knife, but a keyboard and the right person operating it. She aimed a left hook at Vokov and Donovan's smiling faces. *And I am the greatest.*

Chapter Twenty-Eight

Three Weeks Later

Trigger sat next to Storm at the team table in the busy downtown bar. A regular weekly meetup when Alpha team was home. Seated with his back to the wall, he nursed a sweating bottle of bear and wondered why the hell he was doing there. A thought he'd had several times over the past three weeks.

In a series of WTF moments, he had allowed Mary to convince him to return to Manhattan, and again tonight, when she insisted they join Sentinel's social night. Hell, he would raze the planet to see her smile.

Fuck knew why Vokov had gone to ground. Not for long, he suspected, but as of now, Hawke had nothing. Aside from Dex, his entire team was present. No one, including their significant others, was fooled by his brothers' relaxed façades. No fool stood a chance if they were stupid enough to make their move.

Comforting. Yeah, nah. As far as he was concerned, the only safe place for Mary and Lucy was inside his home, which, thanks to Hawke, was locked up tighter than Camp David.

Saturday was Open Mic night. They were at the early session, but the bar was packed with people itching to take the stage. Including

Mary. The hairs on the back of his neck stood to attention as he watched her hitch her perfect backside onto the stool and smile at the guy playing piano. The words *sitting duck* sprung to mind.

"Your girl any good?" Storm asked, nudging his arm.

Not my girl. Get over it. Tonight, she ain't leaving with anyone else but you. "Better than good." Truth. He hadn't heard her sing in a long time. Too long.

The tip of her tongue swept her lips. Nervous. She had no call to be. The color of her blue shirt matched her eyes perfectly. They sparkled under the light reflected from the disco ball. Magic. No other word for it—her.

Trigger's breath caught in his throat at the first sound of the ballad's chords. The song they used to belt out on long drives in his truck, back when they had a future.

This past week had been amazing. Making love to her, falling asleep with her wrapped in his arms. Getting to know Lucy. Their daughter, she'd assured him a thousand times. A spot in his dark soul believed her. Why else was the kid calling him dad?

Even if it did turn out they didn't share blood, a fact Mary insisted wasn't true. He didn't care. She was his to care for and protect. The possibility his genes were wrecked beyond redemption meant it would be best if they didn't share DNA.

Mary's voice soared, rich with heartfelt emotion, and his foot tapped to the rhythm of the song under the table. *Our song.*

Maggie, Mia, and Jenna answered her call to come up on stage and sing the chorus. Snake's wife, Sam, had offered to sit with Lucy for a couple of hours while they were there.

Between verses, Mary laughed at something Maggie whispered in her ear. She fit in, as if she had always been a member of their tight-knit group.

Her eyes found his across the crowded bar. Their connection electric, charged with unspoken words and lingering what-ifs. As the lump in his throat grew to mammoth size, peeling the label off his beer bottle fascinated him.

The song reached its end, and the whoops, whistles, and hand clapping made his heart swell. The crowd loved her.

"Damn, your girl's got pipes!" Storm yelled over the noise, slapping him on the shoulder.

His girl. The words reminded him of what he almost lost. What he was terrified of wanting again. Memories crashed over him like a tidal wave. The tears of joy in her eyes all those years ago when he proposed. Promises made, the future they'd planned and lost.

Too much. He stood abruptly, his chair scraping against the floor. "Need some air," he mumbled to no one in particular, already pushing his way through the crowd towards the exit.

As he retreated, he felt her eyes following him, but he didn't look back. He burst out into the cold night air, determined to claw back some distance.

His body faced the parking lot, his truck a few feet away. Winter would see she got home safely, so why didn't his boots get the message?

No matter how hard he struggled to take those steps, he failed. Mary held his heart. Commanded every move he made, and none of them were creating any more distance between them.

***

Wow. Mary turned to Maggie. "That felt great".

"You were amazing. They should offer you a permanent gig."

The smile on her friend's face fell. "What?"

"Where's he going?" Maggie's head tilted to the exit.

"Matt?" Mary called after him, but he didn't seem to hear her over the noise in the bar. She was halfway to the door when Hawke stepped in front of her.

"Hey. You were great, but I don't have long. Come with me. I have the tracker."

Damn. She forgot. Part of the reason she'd been able to convince Trig to come tonight was to get the equipment fitted. "Okay." She shrugged. She'd lost sight of Matt. Figuring he must have gone to the rest room, she followed Hawke in that general direction.

Mary leaned against the cubicle wall, trying to catch a normal breath. Ever since Uncle Jack baled her up in the bathroom all those years ago, tight spaces were a challenge. The fact that Hawke had her hands all over her bra didn't help.

"Cozy, right?" Hawke grinned.

Mary felt her cheeks flush when her next breath shoved her breasts against Hawke's hand.

"This baby is undetectable." Hawke smiled.

Oh my God. Not knowing where to look, Mary raised her eyes to the ceiling as Hawke fastened the hook and eye and broke the attached needle and cotton with her teeth. *Why did I wear a front closing bra? Simple. It gave Matt quick access. Not subtle, but serviceable.* Mary added a smile of her own.

"It will ping your location every fifteen minutes to a secure server."

"That's creepy."

"I guess, but it will keep you safe if you and Trig are separated. Though I can't see him letting you or Lucy out of his sight until Vokov is caught."

"Thanks. I appreciate it, and I don't mean to be rude, but I have to tell Trig something." He couldn't have gone far. They were leaving in a few minutes to go pick up Lucy for dinner at his parents' home.

As if she'd been hit by a tank, she stopped dead in her tracks. How could she be so dumb? He said he didn't want to go, but like a lot of things lately, she'd pushed.

"No problem. I'll come by yours tomorrow and fit the munchkin with something similar. A tiny bird told me Storm may be getting up to sing. Now that I have to see."

Mary nodded, but didn't look back as she went back to the bar. Her heart flip-flopped when she didn't see him anywhere, so she stepped outside. Why the hell was he standing out there, alone in the dark? "Matt? What happened? I know I'm a little rusty, but was I that bad?"

The sudden turn, the way he prowled toward her, frightened her. "Is he here? Vokov. Is he here?" Her breath hitched as he took hold of her arm.

"No. He's not here. You're scaring me. What is it?" Her feet skimmed the ground.

The door opened and music blasted into the street. Matt's arms circled her waist.

"Dance with me."

Instinctively, her body relaxed against the warmth of his body.

"I'm sorry. I needed air. You didn't need to follow me. Vokov's men could be anywhere."

His nose nuzzled her neck, and her skin bristled at the whisper of his eyelashes against her skin.

"I know. Sorry. Your parents?" They needed to leave, but the ache below her navel, the missing him, had started the instant she lost sight of him. Two minutes wouldn't hurt. "It's been a long time since we danced together. I'd forgotten how much I like it."

His smell, fresh pine needles with a hint of campfire smoke, was a dead cert turn on whenever they were up close. Now was no different.

"Let's finish the song." The tip of his tongue swept the inside of her ear.

"We don't want to be late." Honestly, she'd rather go home. Rocking her pelvis against the bulge against his zipper, she prayed like crazy he understood her not-so-subtle message.

Without warning, her feet left the ground, and she was in his arms, heading for the exit.

"Let's go get Lucy and get this over with. Catch you later," he hollered over his shoulder to their table.

Forty-five minutes later, her fingers tightened around Matt's as they walked up the flagstone path to his parents' front door. The tension in his broad shoulders telegraphed his mood. Not happy. "It's not too late. We don't have to do this," she whispered, though Lucy had been looking forward to meeting them. Sue had called three times this week, checking on what they liked to eat, whether she should cook anything special for Lucy.

Matt's jaw clenched. "We're here now."

The door swung open. Sue, she guessed, beamed at them. Her silver-streaked hair curved around her round face in a perfect bob.

"You're here. Come in, come in!" Her gaze immediately dropped to her daughter. "And you must be Lucy. I'm so glad to meet you."

"I can write my whole name without any help," she announced, and without hesitating, stepped forward.

"That's wonderful. I'd love to see. Come and show me. Do you like cookies?"

"Do they have hearts? Mommy makes them with hearts."

Sue's face dropped. "No. They're dinosaurs."

"Perfect." Mary jumped in, not wanting the woman to feel bad before the evening had begun.

"Can daddy and mommy have some, too?"

"Sure thing, honey." Lucy's eyes lit up when Sue nodded and took her hand. "This way."

The genuine warmth in the woman's smile made her heart ache. She clearly wanted the evening to go well.

Mary smiled, reached behind her for Matt's hand, and followed Sue into the kitchen. Wow! The woman had gone all out. The table was set with matching china, and the place smelled amazing. Without waiting for any help, Lucy wiggled her backside onto a chair next to a plate of carefully decorated T-Rex cookies.

Chapter Twenty-Nine

Keep it together. Get through dinner. Mary's gentle touch on his arm anchored him.

Seeing Sue, after so long, sent his mind spinning back to the countless dinners they'd enjoyed before he knew the truth, before he understood that every "you get that from your father" comment had been a lie.

Matt watched her push the plate of iced cookies closer to Lucy. She'd always been good with kids. Bittersweet memories invaded his brain. Bandaging his scraped knees, telling him stories of his "relatives" who'd fought in wars, family medical history, she'd offered that wasn't his.

Lucy took a bite of her cookie. "Do you want to see me write my name now?" Crumbs spilled from her mouth onto her sweater.

"Don't talk with your mouth full, sweetie," Mary said quietly.

"Sorry."

"No harm done." Sue leaned forward and kissed the top of the kid's head.

You're trying too hard. Dammit. No amount of her smiles could wipe away almost two decades of deceit.

Trigger's muscles coiled tight when Robert Mitchell emerged from his study. Years after his retirement, his spine was ramrod straight, his military bearing intact. The man who'd taught him about honor and integrity, been his reason for wanting to enlist, had hidden the biggest secret of Trigger's life.

"Son," Robert said, reaching out his hand.

"Sir." He gave him a stiff nod and sat next to Mary.

He wanted to pull her to him, shield her from the anger threatening to consume him. Instead, he breathed deeply. Big mistake. The familiar scent of pot roast and fresh bread made him want to vomit.

The kitchen was exactly as he remembered—warm yellow walls, copper pots hanging above the island, the window box full of herbs Sue insisted on growing year-round. Lucy reached for another cookie and felt the slight tap of Mary's hand on her hungry fingers.

"You can have more after dinner, sweetie."

Unbelievably domestic, the scene hurt.

"I hope you like pot roast, Mary," Sue said. The cheerfulness in her voice carried an edge. "It was always our son's favorite."

"Not true. Never could stomach it." The words slipped out before he could stop them. He caught Mary's sharp look, but every moment in this house felt like he was being buried alive. Slowly. Shovel by shovel.

Smiling, Robert reached for a damn cookie. "How have you, son?"

"Sir. I am not your son."

"Matt," Mary warned, her eyes flashing to Lucy.

She was right, of course. His misery had no business ruining a child's evening. They settled around the dining room table where they had shared countless family dinners. Trigger stared at his plate. How many times had they commented on his eyes being just like Robert's? How many family anecdotes had they shared, knowing they weren't really his to claim?

"The potatoes are delicious, Sue." Mary tossed the words into the silence.

"Family recipe," Sue replied, then winced at her words.

Trigger stabbed a piece of meat. "Whose family?"

"Help yourself to vegetables." Sue's hands trembled as she picked up the bowl and handed it to Mary. "Lucy, honey, have you started school?"

"Soon." Lucy brightened.

"That's wonderful. You know, when Trigger was your age, he..." Sue cut herself off, the words hanging awkwardly in the air.

Trigger's fork scraped against the china. Every childhood memory felt tainted, every memory suspect. He sensed Mary's concerned gaze raking over him, but he couldn't meet her eyes. She'd want him to let it go, to forgive. But how could he when the foundations of his entire life had been built on lies?

Robert cleared his throat. "Son, we've been thinking. There are some documents—adoption papers, birth records in the attic. We kept them for you, if you'd like them."

Too late. Trigger's chair scraped back. "Now you want to share? After I had to find out from a stranger processing my enlistment paperwork?"

"Please," Sue's voice cracked. "We only wanted to..."

"Protect me. Right." Rage surged through his veins.

"You'll always be our son, Matthew. Nothing will change that for me and Robert."

He couldn't stay here, surrounded by photographs of a family that wasn't his, suffocating under the weight of their lies.

"Maybe we should go," Mary suggested quietly, her hand finding his under the table.

A lifeline. He latched onto her touch, even as part of him wanted to pull away. She deserved better than his damage, his trust issues, his inability to let anyone close.

"Sounds like a great idea. Come on poppet. Time for a story." Matt gathered Lucy into his arms and grabbed a cookie for the ride home. He couldn't get to the vehicle fast enough. Leaving Mary to say their goodbyes, he sat in the truck, seething until she climbed in next to him.

Neither of them said a word as they drove home. Every mile adding to his sense of failure. He'd promised her he'd try, but all he'd done was prove he was still broken.

Trig slammed the front door behind them, the sound reverberating through the quiet, and rattling the damn windows. Covering her daughter's ears with her hand, Mary carried Lucy to bed.

Dinner with Rob and Sue had been like walking into a fucking minefield. He told her going to dinner was a bad idea. For all their sakes, he should have refused to do what Mary wanted. All the social work skills on the planet didn't stand a chance of fixing the rift between him and the people he'd once called mom and dad. No matter how good Mary had been at her job.

Years spent in the military away from them, was intended to bury any idea of playing happy families. Tonight, being in their home, the house he'd grown up in brought it all back, and then some. His mind still reeled from their confession on the day he enlisted. They shared no blood ties. His real folks? A drug addict mother and a murdering asshole of a father.

Consumed with anger, he paced back and forth across the living room. The bottle of Bourbon eyeing him from across the room. He'd been holding off all night, but he was in under his roof now, and he needed a drink. The sound of the alcohol glugging its way into his glass sounded sweet.

"Pour me one while you're at it."

Mary leaned one hip into the side of the couch, that same look of pity in her eyes. The one she'd flashed him when he lashed out at Sue and Rob earlier. "Small or large?"

"May as well make it a double."

She sauntered round the front of the couch and flopped onto the couch. *Oh yeah.* Her chest rose and fell with barely held together breath. They were going to fight. If she wanted the full brunt of his hurt, anger and goddam shame, she wouldn't have to beg.

"They're trying, Matt," Mary said softly.

"Trying? They lied to me my entire life."

"They loved you. They still do."

"Love? Love is honest. Love doesn't hide things." Even as he said it, he knew he was being a hypocrite. Wasn't he hiding parts of himself from her?

His hand shook as he tried to replace the cap on the bottle. Without turning, he wasn't ready to look at her, he knocked back the first shot, before giving the cap a final twist, and taking Mary her drink.

"Do you want to tell me what's going on in that head of yours?" Mary cocked her head to one side and placed the glass on the coffee table.

"No." *But I'm sure you won't let it go.*

"Why?"

No reason, and every goddam one on the planet. "Don't feel like talking about it right now. Have to be up early. Meeting Winter for an early PT session.

"Oh. I see."

Of course she did. She never had any trouble seeing through his bull shit. Calling him on it.

She patted the cushion beside her. "You look like you need a hug. Come and sit with me."

God, he wanted nothing more. His whole body burned to touch her, but she had walked out on him. Just like Sue and Robert, she said sayonara to any chance of them being a real family. Vanished into fucking WITSEC without a word, and he still couldn't get over it.

As for believing the precious little girl, sleeping down the hall, with wide eyes, as blue as her mom's, and a smile that rocked his world was his? It couldn't be true. With genes like his, it shouldn't be true.

Another swig of the bourbon, and he found the courage to look at her. What he saw, he didn't like. Her face was too pale, her shoulders up round her ears, begging for his fingers to release the tension. "Tell me again why you left me."

"Matt, please, I can't do this again."

And why should she? He was pathetic. "One more time, Mary. No lies this time."

"I have never lied to you. Though right now, I'm tempted, because clearly the truth isn't doing it for you."

The flicker of hurt, confusion in her eyes clawed at his insides, but he was in it now, swept up in a shitload of questions that had never had answers. All of them asked long before he ever knew her.

"Six years ago. You left. No explanation. No warning. I went through hell wondering if you were dead or alive. I want you. God help me, I need you more than life itself, but I'm having a real hard time believing it won't happen again."

"Matt, I did not have a choice." Her voice shook.

"What the hell does that even mean? There are always options. Choices. Like trusting me, for one. Telling me what the fuck was going on. Letting me help you, for Christ's sake. Is Lucy mine?" Words kept coming, not caring that they belonged in Lucy's story land. No connection to reality. As if he'd struck her, Mary flinched and rose from the couch.

"I'm not lying, Matt. I…"

With a wave of his hand, he cut her off and didn't let up. "When she was born, you didn't care enough to call. Hell, a text saying, *Congratulations, you're a dad, Mary* would have been good."

"I didn't want you to get hurt. I loved you, still love you." Her lips trembled. "Donovan told me it would be for a short time. Trust me, all I wanted was to keep you and our daughter safe."

Trig shook his head. "You know me. Not the details, but what I did for a living was no secret. I could have protected you. I didn't need you to keep me safe."

Damn it, her whole body was shaking. "Sit down," he growled, reaching for her hand. *She did what she thought right, and what do you know about trust?*

He believed his team had his back, as he had theirs, but after what happened with Rob and Sue. Deep down, he didn't trust anyone, and that included his own fucking DNA.

Looking as though the universe had just fallen on her head, Mary held onto his hand and stared at him, her eyes welling with tears. *What have you done?* "I can't." He raked his fingers through his hair, feeling trapped. He wanted to share the fear that everyone he loved would eventually leave. But the words stuck in his throat. "I can't do this right now."

"Then when?" She fought back tears, and each one felt like a knife in his chest. "Will you ever let me back in, Matt?"

Instead of answering, he grabbed his keys and raced for the door.

"Don't you dare walk away from this."

Matt heard her, but the door slammed shut behind him. In his truck, he banged his forehead against the steering wheel. He loved Mary more than he'd thought possible. His daughter too, and it terrified him. How long before Mary realized he wasn't worth the effort and stopped trying to break through his walls?

Chapter Thirty

MARY SAT THERE, STUNNED, listening to Matt drive away. She loved him—God help her. But it meant nothing if he didn't trust her when she told him how much.

Neither of them deserved a future lying beside each other pretending to be asleep, unable to say what was in their hearts. She didn't want that life, and neither did Lucy.

The glass of bourbon sat untouched on the table, and she was seriously tempted to drink that and the rest of the bottle. It wouldn't help. Slowly, she dragged herself off the couch, crept into the bedroom and started shoving their clothes in the bag. Again.

Tears blurred her vision. *Asshole.* She bit her tongue and screamed the word over and over in her head. Coming to find him was never going to be easy, but somewhere in her Pollyanna brain she'd expected, hoped, he would forgive her.

Is Lucy mine? His words had hit harder than a physical blow. Sinking onto the bed, she put her head in her hands and sobbed. Matt was right. She hadn't trusted him. *He said he didn't want kids.* She was never going to risk Lucy facing the same rejection as she had faced.

Her breath caught in her chest. The past six years in witness protection had been the hardest of her life, and sure there were lonely moments when she wanted to call Matt, to explain, tell him they were

alive and safe. But Frank had been clear—no contact with anyone, including the man she loved.

Sara had warned her. To Matt, she was just another liar, a
person who had betrayed him.

"Mommy?"

The feathery touch of Lucy's fingers made her jump. Mary
gathered her in her arms and hugged her tight. "Sorry, sweetheart." She was a child, who didn't have a clue what was going
on other than mommy was fighting with the man she was calling
daddy. Honestly, she doubted the kid understood more than she
had a new best friend. A buddy for Floppy Hop.

And that was not okay. Because they couldn't put out the
massive bonfire that was their relationship, didn't mean their
daughter had to suffer.

"It's okay, sweetie. We're going on a trip."

"Disney world Is daddy coming, too?"

Mary forced a smile. The kid never gave up. "No sweetie. Just
you and me." No way would she set foot in Manhattan again.

***

All in, Lucy leaned against her leg as she opened the door to her
parents' home. She hadn't stopped crying since she learned they
weren't going to Florida and Matt wasn't coming with them,
either. Her cheeks were red and her eyelids heavy. Poor mite
needed sleep. They both did. She picked her up and cuddled her
close. "We're here, sweetie. This is where mommy grew up."

"With Aunt Sara?" Lucy mumbled over her thumb.

"Yes, sweetie." Mary fumbled for the light switch and waited
for the ancient wiring to hum to life. The house smelled of the
furniture polish her mom had religiously applied to anything
made of wood.

"Want to see mommy's old room?" Thanks to the old floor-
board, no bad guy would sneak up on them in the middle of the
night. But, just in case, once she put Lucy to bed, she'd figure out
their possible escape routes.

Upstairs, her bedroom seemed frozen in time. Faded purple walls, boy band posters The single bed still wore the quilt her grandmother had made, the colors dulled but the stitching intact. She should open a window and let in some fresh air, but she wasn't that brave.

Lucy wriggled from her arms and ran to the closet. Tiny fingers examined the height marks etched onto the neck of the giraffe sticker on the door.

"Is this you, Mommy?" she asked, plastering her back against the leg of the giraffe.

"Yes, sweetie." Mary touched the highest mark. See, MARY 15. The summer before everything changed. Before Uncle Jack. "I don't know about you, but I'm sleepy." She lifted Lucy onto the bed. "Sit here while I fetch our bag and pajamas, then I'll make us a hot chocolate."

"With marshmallows?"

Lucy had made sure she popped the bag on the counter when they stopped for gas. "Sure thing. Now stay here. Won't be long."

"No! Don't leave me." Lucy screamed.

Mary snatched her daughter in her arms and buried her tiny face against her heart. "I'm so sorry, sweetie. Don't be scared. Everything's okay." She leaned back slightly and wiped away her tears. "You can come with me."

"Okay." Lucy jumped off the bed. "When is daddy coming?"

If she could have crawled under the bed and died, she would have. "Did you pack Floppy Hop?" she asked. Anything to distract her.

"Yes. He comes everywhere with us. He's family."

Was there a hint of accusation in her tone? In any case, she ignored the possibility as they went to the car. Quickly. There had been no sign of anyone following them, but how would she know? Matt was the one trained in this stuff. A shiver ran down her spine, convinced the bad guys lurked in every shadow.

It didn't take long to get Lucy into her pajamas and make their hot drink.

"Story?" Lucy asked, clutching Floppy Hop.

Mary curled beside her daughter on the narrow bed, breathing in her strawberry shampoo, and told Lucy's favorite story of the angry dragon and gawilla bites at least twice before she fell asleep.

Alone now, creepier than ever, the house whistled and creaked. In the kitchen, making as much noise as possible, she made herself another cup of hot chocolate. Sitting by the window in her mother's rocking chair, her knee ached. A constant reminder of that god forsaken day.

From here, she could see the full moon high above the trees, casting the same shifting shadows on the wall that had terrified her as a child. Her phone buzzed. Maggie. Again. She'd called several times in the past couple of hours. This time, she'd better answer before her friend organized the search party.

"Trig's looking for you. Are you okay?"

It was good to hear her voice. It felt like they had known each other a long time, when it had only been a few months. "Not sure why. He's an ass?" For the hundredth time that day, she patted her eyes and blew her nose.

"Oh, hon. He knows he was an idiot, but I swear he cares about you and Lucy. I wish you'd heard him talking to Winter. He's sorry. Swears he'll make it up to you. Why don't you answer his calls? Give him a chance?"

"Maggie." Mary's voice cracked. "Being angry at me for disappearing six years ago, I understand, but he asked me if Lucy was actually his?"

"You said it. Ass. Restrained on your part, if you ask me. Why you didn't. Anyway. He knows he screwed up big time, and he's frantic trying to find you. Where are you?"

"At my parents' old house. Which he probably could guess if he had half a brain. But it's too late." She sniffed and sniffed again. Odd. The house was old, funky, but it never smelled like a gas station.

"Mary. What's going on?" Maggie asked.

"I'm not sure. The place smells weird, like smoke. Shivers. Maybe I left something on the stove." *No, you damn well didn't.* The smoke detector shrieked. "I'll call you back." Searching for her next breath, she ran to Lucy. "Wake up, baby."

"Mommy?"

"I'm here, sweetheart." Heart pounding, she scooped her out of the bed, pressed her face against her shoulder, and headed back the way she'd come. Wisps of smoke floated along the hall.

Damn it. She swallowed several times but couldn't stop coughing. Flames liked the curtains. The fire was spreading fast.

"Mommy, I'm scared."

Feeling lightheaded and afraid they didn't have much time before the whole place caved in, the window at the other end of the hall looked like their best option to escape.

Holding her daughter with one arm, she pulled on the latch. Lack of use over the years had rusted it shut. *Smash it.* Possible, but the panes were too small to squeeze through.

We're trapped. To hell with that. Lucy whimpered. "It's okay, baby. Mommy's going to get us out of here." To protect her from the smoke, Mary pulled her pajama top loosely over the child's head, walked inside the guest bedroom across the hall, and shut the door.

"Hang in there, sweetie." This window wasn't like the others in the house. One summer, her dad had replaced it. She couldn't recall why, but she muttered a silent thank you.

Prying Lucy's arms from around her neck, she lowered her to her feet and looked around for something to protect her hand from breaking glass. "Close your eyes, sweetie." Wrapping a pillowcase around her hand, she stepped in front of her baby, shielded her face with her forearm, and punched her fist through the window.

"Okay. You and Floppy Hop ready for an adventure?" Doing her best to avoid the broken glass, she grabbed Lucy and climbed out of the burning house. Once they were on terra firma, she took off for the gate leading to the paddock. Sweat poured from her brow. Acrid smoke stung her eyes., and her leg felt like it would snap, but she wouldn't stop until they were safe.

Behind them, she heard the crunch of tires on gravel. Two men wearing balaclavas, like the man who attacked her at the cabin, ran from the direction of the burning house to meet the black SUV.

Lucy's tiny body quaked in her arms. "We'll be okay, I promise, baby." Gritting her teeth, she hurried along the tree line, trying to stay out of sight, except it ended soon, and then there was nothing but wide, open land.

Think, Mary. The hideout, dad had built for her and Sara when they were kids was up ahead and to the left, nestled high in the branches of an old tree. They had to hurry. What if it hadn't survived? Her heart sank. Except there it was, the cubby house.

This time, when she tried to set Lucy on her feet, she sobbed louder.

"Floppy Hop. I dropped him."

Damn. "Shh, we need to be quiet. Let's play Hide and Seek?" She grabbed her hand.

Lucy looked at her as if she'd gone mad. "I'm sure daddy will be here soon. It's his favorite game. He's probably with Floppy Hop." she lied. *Not.* The irony didn't escape her. "I know the perfect place. Look." With the tip of her finger, she angled the child's chubby cheek toward the tree house. "It's Aunty Sara's secret hiding place."

"Come with me."

Mary kneeled in front of her, cupped her daughter's face in her hands, and brushed away her tears. How many times could a heart break in a day? More than she ever imagined. "I need you to be brave for me, sweetheart, and climb up there and hide. Can you do that?"

Lucy's bottom lip trembled. "Okay."

Sucking in a deep breath, she kissed her tiny hand. "Good girl. Daddy will come and find you soon. Remember. Stay up there until he says the magic words."

"What words?" Lucy whispered.

The faint smile on Lucy's lips broke her heart. Leaving her was the hardest thing she'd ever done, but it was the only way. Hopefully, when the men saw her take off across the paddock, they would chase her and forget about their daughter long enough for Matt to find her. She had to believe he would come for them. "Magic words are Gawilla Bites. Can you remember?"

Lucy rolled her eyes. "Of course. Gawilla Bites."

"Clever girl. Up you go. Hide, sweetheart."

"But Mommy—"

"Go on, now." Her voice faltered. "I'll see you soon."

Her lip trembled, then her brave little girl nodded. "I'm so proud of you, baby." Tempted to pull her in for a hug and never let her go, she popped a quick kiss on her forehead. "I love you so much. Remember, wait for daddy and say the magic words. Okay?"

Once she was safe, Mary wiped her eyes and limped to the edge of the trees. Determined to put as much distance between Lucy and Vokov's men, she picked up her pace.

They were coming. She could hear the rumble of the SUV drawing closer. *Please, Matt. Hurry.* The tracker was still inside her bra, but had Hawke got around to telling him? God, she hoped so. The thought of Lucy spending a freezing night in the treehouse made her feel sick.

Shifting direction, she ran until rough hands gripped her arms and yanked her off balance. Twisting right and left, she tried frantically to rip free, but he was stronger. Another man appeared.

"No!" Mary screamed behind the hand now clamped over her mouth, but a needle prick to her neck brought the darkness. Her last conscious thought was of Matt holding Lucy in his arms. *Safe.*

Chapter Thirty-One

WHY DID HE STAY out all night? Why didn't he keep his big mouth shut? Two of the questions, and there was a lot more rattling through his head. Kicking himself for walking out on them, leaving them unprotected. When a walk round the block should have cleared his mind. Trig checked every room in his damn house. *Pathetic.* He prided himself on being an elite soldier, not a chicken shit.

Dinner with Rob and Sue, *his* parents, at least the only ones he'd ever known, fucked with his head. Led him places he should never have traveled, and now his entire world had up and left him. Who could blame her for wanting to be as far away from him as possible?

His life would not be worth living if anything happened to them. "Lucy. My kid." Saying the words out loud confirmed it not only to him, but to the fucking universe. Breathing deep he let the claim resonate to his core.

After checking a third time, he headed for his truck, not knowing where to start, but he'd search until he found them. Beg Mary to forgive his sorry ass. The sudden chirp of his phone sent his blood pressure skyrocketing. "Mary? Sweetheart?"

"It's Maggie."

"What you got?" He'd rung her as soon as he realized they had left. If anyone knew where they were heading, it had to be Winter's wife.

She and Mary had bonded from the moment she set foot on their doorstep. "Did you find her, is she okay?"

"Easy, big guy. I spoke to her."

"And? What did she say? Should I call her, or..."

"Please, Trig. Shut up and listen."

Maggie sounded scared. Not good. He steeled himself for the inevitable. She wanted nothing to do with him.

"She's at her parents' old place. We were talking when she said she thought she smelled smoke, then her phone went dead."

His blood turned to ice. "When?"

"Minutes ago."

"Shit. Did you try calling her back?"

"What the hell do you think? Of course, I did. No answer."

"Sorry." He raced back to the house, took his weapon from the safe and picked up his Go Bag from the hall closet. "Call the fire department. I'm on my way." He rattled off the address and raced to his truck. "Is Winter with you?"

"Yes."

"Put him on. Please."

"I heard. On my way." Winter said.

"Thanks, brother." Next, he called Snake.

"Talk to me." The boss' voice oozed combat readiness.

"It's Mary. Fire. Her parents' place in Durham, Connecticut."

"What the hell happened?"

"I'll explain later. Right now, I need the chopper."

"Copy that. Head for the heliport. I'll call the farm and let them know you're inbound."

Trigger's Dodge Charger roared to life, tires squealing as he hit the street. When he arrived, Winter was already waiting at the heliport. "Thanks for coming." He squeezed his friend's shoulder, grateful to see him.

"Sure thing. And if I'm not mistaken, that's Storm." He raised his chin. "Looks like Snake is with him."

Trig watched his teammates approached. "Boss?"

"What? Didn't think I'd let you have all the fun?"

"All aboard, gentlemen." The pilot hollered from the cockpit.

An hour later, the man who owned the farm had them parked on Mary's street. Fire trucks, manned with New York's bravest, maneuvered their hoses in various directions, trying to stop the blaze from spreading to the nearby trees.

He took off before anyone stopped him and grabbed the closest firefighter. At the single tap on her shoulder, she faced him. "Anybody, inside?" His voice hitched.

"No. Place is empty."

"Check the perimeter!" Snake swung into action, while Storm activated one of Hawke's drones.

Good thing the boss kept a clear head. When he saw Floppy Hop lying in the grass, he choked and hoped to Christ he found his family alive. He stuffed the soft toy into the pocket of his cargo pants and kept running.

"Hawke." He spoke into the comms they'd activated before leaving the heliport. "You there?"

"Yeah. I'm trying to locate Mary's tracker."

"You're kidding me. You have eyes on them?" Why hadn't she told him? *Probably because she did give her much change, asshat.*

"Give me a minute." Hawke said.

They didn't have that much fucking time. Winter jogged alongside him. It felt good knowing he wasn't alone.

"Gotcha."

He winced at the shriek in his ear. "Where are they?"

"Not sure which one, but my guess is it's the kid. Drone picked her up. Straight ahead, two hundred meters into the trees. Still working on Mary's tracker."

"Hawke, keep your eye on where Mary's heading. Send me coordinates when they stop. Trig, Winter, go find Mary. Storm with me. We'll check the rest of the property." Snake ordered.

"Copy that." Their answer rang out in unison.

"Trig. Through the trees, there's some sort of structure. Lucy's there." Issuing the bearing, Hawke's voice crackled over comms.

"I see it. It's the old treehouse. Checking it out." Trig said, glancing over his shoulder. Keeping pace, Winter nodded.

The kid's hideout sat eight feet above their heads. No sound. No movement until a sudden jerk in the dangling rope ladder. His heart thumped against his chest.

Trig circled the red maple. "Lucy?" A tiny sniffle from above stopped him cold. "Hey, it's dad. You up there?" His whole body tensed as he prayed for an answer.

"I'm scared."

A lump rose to the back of his throat at the sound of her croaky voice. Smoke swam over their heads. He had to get her out of there.

"You're safe, now, poppet. You can come out."

"Mommy said only come out when you say the magic words."

His heart clenched. "Did Mommy tell you the words poppet?"

"Yes. Gawilla Bites."

"That's right. Gawilla Bites. Clever girl."

Teary eyes peered down at him. "Daddy?"

"Yes, sweetheart."

"I need help. I'm stuck."

"No problem, poppet. I'm coming up."

Smudges of gray streaked across her cheeks. *When I get my hands on that mother fucker. Relax.* He sucked in a breath and wiggled his jaw to dislodge the tension building behind his teeth and forced a smile he hoped didn't scare her to death.

Lucy's bottom lip trembled as he leveled with the opening and drew her rescued bunny from his pocket. "Look who I found. Must have got lost."

"Floppy Hop. He was hiding." Tiny hands grabbed her favorite toy, then hooked around his neck. "Thank you."

"My pleasure, poppet. Where's mommy?" He braced for a meltdown.

"Bad men were chasing us. Mommy said stay here." She buried her head against his chest.

His skin chilled as her tears soaked through his shirt. "Hey, don't cry. You did good."

"Mommy," she sobbed.

"Shh." Trig cradled her close. "I've got you, and I'm going to find Mommy."

"Promise?"

"Pinky promise." He linked his large finger with her tiny one. "Now hold on tight." Trig slowly climbed down the ladder. "I need you to go with Winter, poppet. He and Maggie will keep you safe while I go find mommy and bring her home."

Winter tried to take Lucy from his arms, but her grip tightened.

"No. Want to stay with you."

"Hey." He placed her gently on her feet and hooked his finger under her soft chin. "Br brave a little longer, just until I find Mommy, then we can go for ice-cream?"

A small nod. "Okay." She faced Winter, gave him a shy, heart-breaking smile, and reached for his hand.

"That's my girl." Trig placed his hand on Winter's shoulder and leaned in until his mouth was close to his ear. "Guard her with your life."

"Roger that."

"So, what's your favorite flavor ice-cream?" Winter asked as he scooped Lucy into his arms.

Trig pulled his mic closer. "Lucy secure. Winter has her. Where's Mary?"

Chapter Thirty-Two

FOCUS. WAKE UP. SEATED in the middle of the space, her arms were bound with zip ties to a chair that swayed when she moved. A dirty piece of rag covered her mouth, and her throat was dry from lack of water and whatever drug they used to knock her out.

On three sides of the vast warehouse, thin shards of sunlight filtered through the broken windows and landed on pieces of rusty machinery. Littered with broken glass, the rotting floor reeked of rot and mildew.

There was a huge broken skylight above her head, and the roof looked close to collapse. The space hadn't been an active business in years. Oddly, the graffiti scrawled over the walls gave her hope the taggers might return and call the cops.

Cataloguing her surroundings kept her mind off the nausea. The last thing she wanted to do was vomit into the gag and end up choking herself. A sitting duck, Mary tried not to waste time guessing through which door the next threat would come. Counting to ten, she willed her growing hysteria to punch down a notch or two.

Visible through the open heavy doors at one end shone the lights of the Manhattan skyline. How long had she been here? A day, more. *Oh, God, Lucy.* Tears rolled down her cheeks. Was she cold, hungry?

Her kid was tough, but what if she tried to climb out of the tree house? She might fall. *Please, Matt, find her.* She whispered the words as Vokov prowled into the warehouse. Beside him, another man carried a chair which he placed in front of her.

Vokov straddled his chair and untied the gag. His eyes were as black as the hair pulled into a man bun at his nape. She bit her bottom lip until she tasted blood. Equal parts terrified and mad as hell, she wouldn't give him the satisfaction of seeing her cry.

The rag digging into the side of her mouth didn't make it easy, but she managed a yawn. Vokov moved swiftly, half rising from his chair and smacking her in the mouth.

Blood trickled over her chin. Staring straight ahead, she stared at the lights of the city as the pain in her jaw spread across her cheek to her ear.

"At last, Ms. Lane, we meet face-to-face."

Her eyes remained locked on the broken glass around her feet as a wave of nausea rolled through her body.

"I've had plenty of time to think about my brother's last moments. You remember, Victor?" Vokov untied the rag from her face and used it to dab her lips.

Was it best to pretend she had no clue who he was talking about or apologize for something she wished could happen again? As neither was likely to gain her any kudos with the monster, she stayed quiet.

"You don't remember. Victor?"

"Please." Please what? She wasn't sure. Please elaborate, please forgive me, please let me go. Her heart clenched.

"My younger brother. The one you murdered."

Vokov's spit hit her in the face right before he slapped her again. Just for fun this time. As the chair wobbled, she braced for the fall, but he caught her arm.

"Maxim was my family. Did you think about that when you called the cops?"

"He was an animal. A sex trafficker who tried to kidnap a teenage girl," she slurred, and looked him in the eye, daring him to hit her again. His hand gripped her jaw, long fingernails digging into her cheek.

"An eye for an eye, Ms. Lane. I am going to kill your daughter," he whispered in her ear.

"Leave her alone," Mary pleaded, her heart pounding. "She's only a child."

"Yes, it's a pity that a little girl has to pay for her mother's mistake." He released her face and straightened his tie.

"Kill me if you want revenge." Her breath hiccupped in her throat.

Vokov grinned and adjusted his cuff. "Oh, I have every intention of ending your life, Ms. Lane, but first you'll watch your daughter die."

"Go to hell. You're a monster, who..." The back of his hand caught her mid-rant.

Vokov nodded, and a man she hadn't noticed before stepped out of the shadows. A syringe in his hand. "No. Please, you don't need to drug me. I'm tied to a chair, you moron." Damn. Why did she have to sound so desperate when she wanted to kill? *Think of Lucy. Safe. Hidden.* Through the pain, her mind played tricks, flashing memories of Lucy's first steps, her giggles, the way she scrunched her nose the same way Matt did when she was thinking.

"As you wish." He waved the man away. "Tell me where she is, and I'll make her death quick. Wait for me to find her and I'll let my friend here spend a few hours with her. He's very fond of little girls."

Fire raged through her veins, summoning every ounce of defiance she had left. "Go to hell," she screamed.

"You, first."

The other man gripped her hair and yanked her head back, forcing her spine to arch. He held her steady, laughed when Vokov reached over the back of his chair and licked the top of her breast. Mary's whole body shuddered. Gritting her teeth, she told herself she didn't care. He could rape and beat her if that got him off, because the longer it took for him to find Lucy, there was a chance Matt would find her first.

"Exquisite." Vokov licked his lips. "I understand why your hero finds it hard to let you go."

Oh, God. Watching him pull the lighter out of his pocket sent her heart rate through the roof. His sneer was a giveaway, but she refused to let her mind go there, until he lit the cigarette and pressed the tip to her forearm. "You son of a bitch." The man holding her hair loosened his grip and pushed her chin to her chest.

Vokov kicked the leg of the chair. Mary hit the ground with enough force to crack ribs and drive the air out of her lungs.

"Get her up."

Bile rose to the back of her throat as the other man hurled her upright.

"Where is she?"

Vokov's slap to the top of her head reverberated through her body. The blow sending daggers through her injured ribs.

"Careful *myshka*. You don't want to kill her before you have what you want."

Her vision was blurry, but she recognized the voice of the man walking towards them. "Frank?". The person she'd trusted with her life. "Why?" she whispered. Pain lanced through her side.

"Love, Mary. It is a powerful motivator. But you know this.

"Lucy thought the world of you," she choked and drew back her shoulders. "Drop dead. Both of you." Blood oozed from her wrists where the zip ties bit into her wrists. Every breath sent a sharp pain through her rib cage, but she would never give in to this monster.

"Believe it or not, Mary, I regret seeing you like this. I would have preferred to forget about you and move on, but family ties cut deep?" Frank shook his head.

Sad fact. If they only knew. Faced with the reality she might never see Lucy again, it was impossible to stop her tears. Vokov reached for his buzzing phone.

"Your boyfriend is becoming quite the inconvenience." He grabbed her chin, fingers digging into her jaw.

"He's coming for you. Both of you." The words earned her another backhand. Stars exploded behind her eyes. *So worth it.* She smiled when the chair rocked, but didn't fall.

"But he won't find you in time, little mouse."

Chapter Thirty-Three

Trig leaped from the bird. His feet barely touched the ground as he raced to his truck.

"I'll drive." Storm stated.

Grateful his friend offered no room to argue, he aimed for the passenger side. Add mad as hell to scared witless and he was in no fit state to drive. He needed time to sort his shit before they reached Mary's location.

Hawke had located Mary while they were in the air and the boss had her on comms as he hopped in the back of the vehicle. Storm hit the gas, and the Charger's engine roared to life.

Trig checked his weapon. He knew these men almost as well as he knew himself. Together, they would bring Mary home. Breaking the promise he made to Lucy had no place in his reality. Not in this lifetime.

Hang in there, sweetheart. Right now, he wasn't sure she wanted anything to do with him, except she had told Lucy to wait for him. She must believe he'd come for her, too.

"Talk to me, Hawke. What are we walking into?" Snake asked.

"Thank fuck her signal stabilized. A disused warehouse close to the Yonkers Pier. Sending tactical approach vectors now."

Trig angled his body to the back seat and noted the detailed intel scrolling on Snake's tablet as he checked schematics and access.

"There are three main buildings." Hawke continued. "Looks like our girl is on the ground floor."

"Any idea of the number of hostiles?" Trig pushed, eager to know what the hell they were up against.

"Hard to tell, but heat signatures show... Hate to say this, but someone is on the ground."

Mary. "Alive?" His hands shook.

"Focus, friend," Storm prompted.

"S'okay, I got this." The words caught in his throat. "Vital signs?"

"Present. Whoever they are, they're alive."

"Thoughts on access?" Snake asked.

"All exits are guarded. But there's a partially collapsed catwalk running the length of the roof. Back in the day, would have been used for maintenance access. I'd suggest, rappel from there, and enter through the skylight. Most likely broken."

"Sightlines?" Storm added.

"There is a water tower that gives optimal sniper coverage of the entire east side. Sam is on her way with her dogs to meet Winter at his house. He says to tell you once Lucy is secure, he will head straight to you."

Trig breathed easier, knowing Winter with his scary sniper shit was on the way. Sam, Snake's wife, was an ex-military K9 handler with skills as lethal as their own. His kid couldn't be in more capable hands.

"Status on their comms?" Snake checked.

"Standard encrypted channels 101." Hawke chuckled. "Thanks to the backdoor I planted in Vokov's network, I can kill their communications the second you give the word."

"That's my girl." Snake nodded.

"Hey, watch your language." Hawke grumbled.

"Apologies. My bad. Any timelines to be aware of?" Snake rolled his eyes.

"Working off their current cycle, the next guard rotation ought to be at zero-one hundred. Two men on staggered patrols. I imagine the way Storm must be driving you'll make that, so let me create a blind spot for insertion."

By the time they parked a klick away from the disused warehouse, his warrior mask was in place. The familiar final check of his gear and weapons sealed in place the confidence he relied on to get through the next thirty minutes.

Mary's face, the hurt in her eyes when he'd questioned Lucy's paternity, flashed in front of him. "Forgive me. Deep down, I always knew." The words escaped before he could stop them.

"Knew what?" Storm rose to his full height after securing his ankle blade.

"That Lucy was mine," he snarled. "I let old ghosts make me doubt it. It's my fault that Mary is in there, hurt, or worse. I should never have walked away."

"Hey." Snake's voice carried the authority not only of their team leader but of years of friendship. "You want to beat yourself up? Do it later. Right now, she needs you square in the middle of this game."

"Roger that."

"Storm, take up position at the water tower until Winter arrives. I'll approach from the west, through what looks like the old admin offices. Trigger, as Hawke suggested, you make your way across the catwalk and rappel through the skylight. That puts you closest to that stationary heat signature."

A resounding "copy that" echoed from him and Storm. Trigger secured his harness. *Game on.*

"Best get a hustle on, guys. They could be prepping for transport." Hawke chimed in over the comms.

"Like hell they are. Snake, we need to go," he said, his heartbeat starting to race.

"Okay. You know what to do. Nobody's taking her anywhere." Snake glanced at his watch. "Hawke, kill power at zero-one-hundred."

"Will do," she confirmed.

"That gives us maximum darkness and shift-change confusion. Trig, once you're in place. I'll breach while you grab Mary."

If Winter didn't make it soon, it was the three of them. Risky. "Vokov dies tonight." Trig eyeballed his teammates.

Snake nodded. His expression glacial. "Questions?"

"Yeah." Storm grinned. "Can we hurry this up? I'm over this asshole messing with our family. Tom has a math exam the day after tomorrow, and I promised to give him a few pointers."

Right. They chuckled. Their brother had fallen hard and fast for the team doc, Jenna. A single mom. Built a strong bond with her teenage son, but their bud was no fucking Einstein.

"Hawke, as always, you're our eyes. Don't let anything surprise us," Snake ordered.

"Please." Her scoff rang with professional pride. "I've got thermal, motion sensors, and three satellite feeds. I'd know if a mouse sneezed. Mary has held out this long. She knows you'll come, Trig."

"Should never have left."

"Hey, man." Storm's grin carried over comms. "When this is done, you're gonna need a ring."

His lips curved. "Already have one. Let's go get my girl." Mary was his. Lucy, too. He'd show no mercy to anyone who tried to take them from him.

"Twelve-fifty-two. Guards approaching rotation points," Hawke confirmed just as Winter powered out of the shadows.

Wasting no time, Snake re-jigged the game plan. "Winter, sniper position at the water tower." He indicated the spot on his screen. "Storm. With me. Let's go."

Night vision goggles in place, Trigger made his way along the edge of the catwalk and prepared for descent.

On cue, the lights went out and the warehouse door blew inward with a thunderous crash. Thanks to the several smoke grenades Snake tossed into the warehouse, he descended like a ghost, unseen until it was too late. He searched for Mary.

A twitch of movement to his left had him pivoting on his back heel to face the threat. A figure emerged from behind a stack of crates, gun firing. Trigger dropped, rolled, and returned the shots. One-two-three rounds, center mass into the US Marshal who had betrayed his woman.

"Myshka!"

Fuck me. Trig turned just in time to avoid the Taiga Machete slicing into him. The blade missing his carotid artery by less than an inch.

Vokov recovered and circled him. Tears looked out of place in the expression of pure rage on his face.

"Shoot the fucker." Snake calmly ordered in his ear.

Behind eyes that no longer saw the world in any true form, Vokov grunted like a pig. Head lowered, he charged again, and he cheerfully fired the shot.

Vokov piled on top of his lover's body, his expression turning from unearthly rage to stunned emptiness. In less than a minute, Mary's torturers were no more. "Yeah. Over too soon for me, too, mother fucker."

"Some people have all the goddam fun." Winter's laugh echoed over the comms. "Should have stayed home and ate ice-cream with my new friend."

"Mary!" Trig called out. Where the hell was she? A muffled sound filtered through the clearing smoke. Tied to a chair, face bruised and bloody. The beautiful blue eyes he'd fallen in love with years ago were glassy and unfocused.

"I'm here, sweetheart." He holstered his weapon. "Stay with me, baby. Stay with me."

"Lucy?" she whispered.

"We have her. She's safe." He sliced through the zip ties with his knife and caught her as she slumped forward. Her breathing was shallow and labored. Judging by the way her hands immediately hugged her torso, he suspected broken ribs. "I've got you."

Her moans as he lifted her into his arms slew him. Blood from cuts on her face soaked into his shirt. Bruising severe enough to close one eye made him want to kill Vokov again for daring to lay his hands on her.

"Matt..." She clutched at his tactical vest.

"Don't talk." He pressed his lips to her temple. Storm rushed to his side. "Stay with me, baby. Please stay with me." Her hand slid from his shirt.

Epilogue

The cabin was quiet, save for the occasional creak of the floorboards and the whistle of the wind finding its way through the snow-covered tree branches.

Trig had used every persuasion technique he knew to convince Mary his apartment was a better place for her to rest and recover, but she insisted the place he had built for them was where she wanted to be.

Storm and Winter had chopped firewood to last the rest of the winter and brought enough blankets to kit out an entire hospital. He pulled the beanie Maggie had knitted him further over his ears. She'd knitted one for Mary and Lucy, even one for Floppy Hop. Lucy loved them, so he guessed he had little chance of taking it off until summer.

It had been a long couple of weeks. Weeks that felt like years. His world had shifted three-hundred-and-sixty degrees the day Mary came back into his life and almost ended when he thought he'd lose her.

Seeing her lying unconscious in the hospital, bloodied and broken, there had been moments where the air in his lungs threatened to desert him forever. But she was here now. Home. And he was never letting her out of his sight again.

His heart swelled listening to her, showing Lucy how to operate the headlamp he'd bought for her. Stepping onto the porch, he took a deep breath, letting the fresh air fill his lungs, and did his best to quell the fragments of fear that still crept in whenever he thought she might leave.

"You, okay, son?"

His hands curled into fists. A reflex he was fighting to control. His stepdad sat in one of the Adirondacks, arms folded, beer by his side, looking into the fire pit. His stepmom had stayed in the city, saying they needed time.

He had to admit they had been a godsend, looking after Lucy while he stayed by Mary's bedside, but the sense of bitterness and betrayal refused to leave him. He'd been struggling to find the right words. The forgiveness Mary assured him was hiding somewhere in his heart.

Trig sat beside him and reached into the snow for one of the beers Robert had stacked beside him. "Mary is doing fine," he said, knowing it wasn't an answer to the man's question, but he didn't want to lie.

Could he be the man Mary wanted him to be and forgive? Certainly, the past couple of months with her and Lucy in his life he had changed him in ways he couldn't explain. Forced him to take a long, hard look at what the word family meant.

"Throw another log on that fire, boy." Robert jerked his chin at the pit.

The heat coming from the flames was powerful, no need for more fuel, but he did as he asked, figuring words beat silence and activity dispersed the heavy atmosphere if only for a few seconds.

Just before his stepdad arrived yesterday, Mary had warned him if he didn't figure out a way round his stubborn pride, he'd regret it. She stopped short of saying his daughter deserved grandparents, but he'd read between the lines. Or was light dawning in that dark spot in his heart?

He took a swig of the long neck, angled his body toward Robert, and did his damndest to knock the chip off his shoulder. "I want us to make this work. For Lucy's sake. And for Mary's."

"I see. And what about you? Does Matthew have anything to say about this?"

Robert met his gaze. There was a flicker in his eyes, something old and familiar that softened spots inside him. Places he had concreted over the day he'd learned of his adoption. "Why?" Trig asked, his voice raw. "Why did you lie to me for so long?"

Robert's shoulders sagged, and he felt as though he'd given the man hope he was about to rip away.

"We thought we were protecting you. In the beginning, your birth mother couldn't take care of you, but she never gave up wanting you in her care. But it would never be possible. Not according to doctors or the law. Later, we were afraid that if you knew, you'd want to find her, put yourself at risk. As the years went by, it became harder to tell you. Your mom and I were afraid of losing you."

Trig tossed another log onto the fire and forced down the old anger still reaching for the surface. "When I found out. I felt like my entire life was a lie. Like I couldn't trust anything or anyone."

"I know, and that's on us. We made a mistake, Matthew. A terrible mistake. But seeing who you are today, the love you have for Mary and Lucy, the father you are, I'm so proud of you, son. And I'm so sorry we ever made you doubt your place in our family."

Trig gulped. The past couple of days he'd shed that many tears, his fucking eyes were red. "Mary believes I can, but I'm not sure I can forgive and forget." Robert nodded.

"Neither me nor your mom expects you to, but can we take it slow, for Lucy's sake, if nothing else?" Robert heaved himself out of the chair and extended hand. "What do you say?"

Trig stood too, the tight knot in his chest loosening as he reached out and clasped his dad's hand. No matter how hard he resisted, the truth was Robert and Sue were the only parents he'd ever known, and they had never stopped loving him.

Silence stretched between them for a few moments before he pulled Robert in for a man hug. Their hands clapped each other's shoulders. A beginning. Enough for now. Trig pulled away and glanced toward the cabin.

"Go take care of your family. I'm gonna have me another beer." Frank sat back down in his chair.

"Steak for dinner?" Trig asked. His dad loved it blue.

"Sure thing. I'll be on my way back to your mom in the morning."

"Appreciate you coming." Heavy words. Words he meant, even if he couldn't follow them up with anything more meaningful just now.

As he stepped into the house, the soft sound of Lucy's giggles echoed down the hallway. "I don't care what your daddy says, you've had enough gawilla bites of chocolate to last a whole week." Mary's playful tone lightened the surrounding air. This, they, were his everything.

When he reached the bedroom, his eyes landed on them straight away. The soft glow of candlelight flickering across the bedroom cast warm shadows on Mary, who sat on the bed, her long, blonde hair tumbling over her shoulders. Lucy sat next to her, holding a Hershey's kiss over her head, while the other gripped her storybook.

"Hey, you." Mary's voice soothed his raw nerves.

The bruises were fading, and she was struggling to keep her spine straight and keep pressure off her healing ribs.

"Come and sit with us. Tell your daughter she has had enough kisses for one day." She patted the spot beside Lucy.

"Never. No one can have too many kisses." He bent his arms and raised his hands in front of him, pouncing on the bed beside his daughter.

"Daddy."

Her muffled cries as he kissed every inch of her tiny body softened the air to where he could take in the huge breath he'd been craving all day. His eyes caught Mary's, his gaze promising the same for her, and more, once they were alone.

"Daddy, stop," Lucy shrieked.

Mary smiled. Despite the shadows lingering under her eyes, he could tell she craved the intimacy as much as he lived for it. He brushed his palm over Lucy's soft hair. Mom and daughter. They were the most beautiful thing he'd ever seen.

"I'm sorry." The words felt heavy, almost impossible to push back the growing lump in his throat. "For everything, Mary. For doubting you... for not being there when I should have been. For not trusting you." He glanced at his daughter. Oblivious, she sat between them, flicking through the pictures in her book as he continued to stroke her hair.

Mary reached for his other hand. "You were scared, Matt. We both were. I'm sorry for leaving you, but you do believe me?" She glanced at their daughter, her voice breaking.

For a moment, he couldn't speak, before it hit him like a gigantic wave. He'd spend the rest of his life proving it to her, if that's what it took. "Yes. With all my heart."

A tear slipped from the corner of her eye as she reached for his cheek. "Good. Be here. Be here with us."

He nodded, his throat tightening as he leaned in to kiss her forehead.

"Hey." Lucy's sweet face popped up between them.

"You need something, poppet?" He grinned as Mary's fingers intertwined with his. Lucy shifted into his lap, and he reached his long arm out to gather both his girls close. "Stay with me," he murmured, hoping Mary would hear him.

"Always, plus a day." She leaned across and whispered in his ear.

Home. Here with them. That was all he needed. "I love you." Above Lucy's head, he kissed her on the lips.

"I love you, too." Mary kissed him back.

"Me, too, daddy. Will you read me a story?"

About the author

LOVE TAKES COURAGE

Eliza writes Romantic Suspense featuring alpha protectors and the strong partners who win their hearts. She is a card-carrying rain lover who enjoys walking on the beach, gardening, and eating ice cream when it pours. When she is not in the editing cave or listening to her characters, she spends time trying her hand at many different crafts, none of which she has mastered. When all else fails you will find her binge watching on Netflix.

Eliza thinks the best part of being a writer is visiting make-believe worlds and falling in love with her next book boyfriend while others stress over parking spaces, their boss, or the cost of a cup of coffee.

I hope you enjoyed Mary and Trig's story as much as I enjoyed bringing them to their happy ending. You can read books one and two in the series on all leading retail platforms. If you would like to meet the original Sentinel team then Books 1 – 3 of the London Series are also available. Check my website for more information. https://www.elizarenton.com

I will be trying something a little different for my next series and venturing into the Paranormal. I love me a good, shape-shifting wolf. Hopefully, I will do them justice. Sign up for my newsletter if you want to know more.